Hope & Sensibility

P. O. Dixon

Hope and Sensibility

Copyright © 2014 by P. O. Dixon

All rights reserved, including the right to reproduce this book, in whole or in part, in any form whatsoever.

This book is a work of fiction. The characters depicted in this book are fictitious or are used fictitiously. Any resemblance to actual events, locales, or persons, living or dead, is entirely coincidental.

Cover Image Photo © Steve Liptrot | Dreamstime.com

ISBN-13: 978-1500515065
ISBN-10: 150051506X

Acknowledgments

Having borrowed many of the much-beloved literary icons from *Pride and Prejudice* and sketched their characters according to my own purposes, I bestow my sincerest gratitude to Miss Jane Austen. I also wish to acknowledge and thank the Jane Austen Fan Fiction community for having the curiosity to ask, "What if?" Many thanks to my lovely beta readers, Regina, Gayle, and Betty for giving of your time to help make *Hope and Sensibility* a delightful reading experience. Your generous support means so much to me.

Foreword

If you have read and enjoyed *He Taught Me to Hope*, you will recall the story ended with a lovely little epilogue, which told of the Darcys' happily ever after: how Darcy's love for Ben was as great as if they were of the same blood, and how he had given Ben more than a home; he had given him a loving family such as Ben truly had never known.

I supposed at the time that was the end of the story. So many of Ben's adoring fans insisted otherwise—you know who you are. Your ardent voices rang loud and clear, and I listened.

During the 2013 National Novel Writing Month (NaNoWriMo), I commenced crafting a new adventure for the adorable young knight who captured the hearts and the imagination of so many. With heartfelt gratitude, I offer you the fruit of my efforts.

Follow along with Darcy, Elizabeth, and Ben as they embark upon a new journey that starts in Derbyshire, carries them to Kent and Hertfordshire, and then finds them once again at Pemberley, their beloved home.

It was such a pleasure revisiting old friends and acquaintances. My fondest wish is that you will enjoy reading this story as much as I delighted in writing it for you.

Table of Contents

Chapter 1	1
Chapter 2	9
Chapter 3	15
Chapter 4	28
Chapter 5	33
Chapter 6	40
Chapter 7	53
Chapter 8	66
Chapter 9	75
Chapter 10	84
Chapter 11	96
Chapter 12	105
Chapter 13	109
Chapter 14	115
Chapter 15	120
Chapter 16	126
Chapter 17	135
Chapter 18	145
Chapter 19	152
Chapter 20	159
Chapter 21	167
Chapter 22	174
Chapter 23	179
Chapter 24	183
Chapter 25	188
Chapter 26	198
Chapter 27	210

"There is no charm equal to tenderness of heart."

Jane Austen

Chapter 1

Absent was the customary spring in his step when young Ben wandered into Darcy's empty study. Affectionately hailed as Sir Lancelot by everyone who knew him best, the little fellow climbed into a chair beside the fireplace. After gazing intently at the roaring flames for a good long while, he sighed.

Darcy's unhurried entrance interrupted his son's musings. "Ben, I thought you were spending the morning with your mother."

"I just came from seeing Mama."

"Did you enjoy a pleasant visit?"

"Mama is sad, and nothing I would say or do made it any better." The little fellow had always taken it upon himself to make his mother smile.

Darcy sat down in the comfortable chair next to Ben. "Son, you must trust that, in time, things will be just as they ever were with your mother."

"I know you say that, and I am sure it is true, but nothing has been the same since our family took their leave of Pemberley. Mama was ever so happy then."

"Indeed, she was. That was a very happy time for all of us."

"So, is such sadness to be expected every year after Christmas?"

"There is something to be said for feeling forlorn at this time of year."

"I shall not rest until I find a way to brighten Mama's day and bring a smile to her face."

"I am sure you shall accomplish your mission." Recalling the events of the past month, Darcy said, "Pray no more surprises like the great scheme of inviting our entire family here at Christmas."

"What was the harm? Everything worked out for the best, did it not?" Ben's countenance clouded. "Well, almost everything. Mama's sadness is not what I had hoped for."

Darcy sympathised with Ben in feeling sad for his mother, for he too was disheartened over Elizabeth's low spirits. He could not confide in Ben the true reason for Elizabeth's sadness. She had been so excited over the holidays when all the evidence of what she was feeling taught her to believe there would be a new addition to their family. Just a week after the last of their family party left Pemberley to return to their own home, Elizabeth's discovered that her fondest wish during the Christmas season was not to be.

"Do you know what is weighing on Mama's spirits? Is there something other than our family's leave-taking?"

"Actually, Ben, there is a far weightier matter that concerns your mother, but, as I said, all will be as it ever was in due time. Pray you will not continue to worry. While I am certain your mother would be pleased to know how much you want to help, she will not be pleased to know how sad you are. She wants you to be happy."

Ben looked out the window. The sun beaming off the snowy landscape flooded the room enough to make his eyes squint. His expression brightened. "I know exactly what will bring a smile to Mama's face this morning. I shall gather Aunt Georgiana, and you must encourage Mama to sit by her window overlooking the maze garden."

Darcy entered Elizabeth's room bearing the tea service he commandeered from the maid in the hallway.

She looked up from her book. "What a pleasant surprise. I did not know you were joining me for tea."

Smiling, he walked over to the table and placed the tea service down. "Indeed. Come, let us sit by the window."

"I do not want to sit by the window."

Darcy strode across the room and drew open the shade. Georgiana and Ben were already busy at work. "Pray reconsider. You will not regret it for it is much pleasanter here by the window. The newly-fallen snow is spectacular. Come sit with me and enjoy the view."

Darcy walked over to the bed and retrieved Elizabeth's comfortable robe. He held it out invitingly and silently urged her acquiescence.

"You are very determined this morning. What are you about?"

"You shall know soon enough."

Elizabeth set her book aside and threw off the covers. Darcy assisted her in donning her robe. While doing so, he placed a light kiss on the side of her neck. After lingering a moment or two to enjoy her affectionate husband's ardent attentions, Elizabeth walked over to the window, prepared to behold the beautiful winter wonderland—Pemberley's magnificent landscape draped in snow. After what seemed liked days of snowfall, it had finally ceased.

Her eyes widened. What a beautiful sight greeted her, and a surprising one as well as she beheld an unexpected, but rather engaging, prospect. Georgiana and Ben were frolicking in the glistening snow and enjoying themselves immensely.

Darcy prepared Elizabeth's favourite tea, just as she liked it: sweetened with a dash of spice and a single lump of sugar. His fingers swept against hers when he offered her the cup.

She cradled the steaming hot beverage with both hands as if relishing the cup's warmth. "Thank you, my love." She took a sip, and then made known her satisfaction with a warm smile. Her eyes fixed outside, she said, "If I might venture a guess, I would say this is the reason you were so adamant in insisting that I sit by the window."

Darcy leaned forward and kissed his darling wife atop her head. "Indeed. Ben felt you needed a bit of liveliness to brighten your day."

"What a thoughtful gesture that was. It is just like Ben to worry about my spirits. However, I wish he would not suffer the burden of attending to my happiness."

"Those are my sentiments precisely, for such is my goal in life. I fear I have failed you, my love."

"No ... on the contrary. I could never wish for a more attentive husband."

Not desiring to make light of a matter that he attributed to his wife's disheartenment of late, and certainly not wanting to add to her woes, he carefully weighed his next words. "I am as eager as you are to expand our family." He traced his thumb along her cheek. "I am very eager. It is just that I do not wish for you to think that begetting Pemberley's heir is my principal consideration."

Elizabeth placed her porcelain cup aside and returned her gaze to the happenings outside her window, thus giving Darcy to know this was not something she wished to deliberate. At length, he tore his eyes away from her, and he peered out the window as well. By now, Georgiana and Ben had noticed them standing there, and they appeared to be trying to garner their share of attention. Elizabeth waved. Ben subsequently jumped up and down, joyfully flailing his arms all about, beckoning Darcy and Elizabeth to join them.

Elizabeth turned and met Darcy's attentive scrutiny. "What do you think? Shall we brave the frightful outdoors and show those two how to fashion a proper ball of snow?"

"Are you certain, Elizabeth? I do not wish to see you overtaxed."

"Indeed, I am quite sure." Her voice filled with playfulness that, to Darcy's delight, now shone in her eyes. "Is that hint of reluctance on your part your way of suggesting that you have no interest in such diversion? How long has it been since you last frolicked in the snow?"

Darcy gave his waistcoat a sharp tug and jutted his haughty chin. "The master of Pemberley does not frolic, madam."

Elizabeth placed her hand upon his chest and started fingering his buttons. "In the snow perhaps, but I declare I have known you to frolic in this very room as well as your own, or has it been so long ago that you have forgotten?"

He took her hand in his and brought it to his lips. "How could I possibly forget, regardless of the passage of time? My nights spent frolicking with you in these rooms constitute some of the happiest moments of my life."

Elizabeth graced him with that beguiling smile that never failed to warm his heart. "Now that we have established that the master of Pemberley has been known to frolic, what say you to joining Georgiana and Ben outside?"

"If you truly want to do this, I suppose there will be no harm. The three of you will likely benefit from my supervision."

"If I know anything at all about Ben's power over you, you will be doing far more than supervising."

"Indeed, that is a sound assertion." Darcy pursed his lips. "I shall make certain to summon assistance from one of the footmen."

Elizabeth lovingly rapped him on his chest. "You would not dare. And should you indeed carry out your scheme, I shall incite a fierce snowball combat that pits Georgiana, Ben and me against you and your footman."

Darcy held up his hands in feigned admission of defeat. "Heaven forbid that should happen." His intention of quitting the room evident, he said, "Shall I wait for you downstairs?"

"Yes, I must arm myself for battle. Shall we say fifteen minutes?"

Elizabeth and Darcy happened upon Ben and Georgiana in time to see the former lying flat on his back, with his arms and legs outstretched and moving back and forth. Georgiana barely contained her enthusiasm. When Ben saw his parents approaching, a warm smile brightened his face. Young Ben jumped up and dashed to Darcy and Elizabeth.

"Mama, Da!" He shook most of the snow from his mittens and slipped his hands into either of theirs. Pulling them along, he said, "You must have a look at what I have done for Aunt Georgiana." Ben's eyes were full of pride over his accomplishment as his family marvelled over his angelic masterpiece.

Doing everything to brush away as much snow from her son's clothing as she could, her manner awash with love and affection, Elizabeth said, "Ben, it is simply amazing. I am certain I have never seen anything as wonderful as this. Where did you learn to do such a thing?"

Ben diverted his eyes to Darcy, who placed a finger to his lips in a manner intended to encourage him not to give away their secret. The fact is that Darcy had taken Ben out of doors just the evening before, and the two of them had made quite an adventure of dishevelling the pristine, newly fallen snow.

Darcy darted his eyes in the direction of the fruit of Ben and Georgiana's earlier endeavours. "If I might hazard a guess, I would say the two of you were crafting a rather oddly shaped snow creature. Why did you abandon your efforts?"

Georgiana said, "We decided it was an arduous task for the two of us, but now that Elizabeth and you are here, what say we resume where we left off, Ben?"

Requiring only the slightest bit of encouragement, Ben raced over and started piling fistfuls of snow upon the rotund heap. After a few moments, he looked back at the others, who seemed perfectly content merely to admire his hard work. "Why are the three of you standing there? Mr. Peters is not going to build himself."

Caught by surprise, Darcy and Elizabeth exchanged questioning glances before looking back at their son, and then spoke in harmony. "Mr. Peters?"

Elizabeth said, "Ben, dearest, wherever did you happen upon that name?"

Young Ben pointed at the bulging mound of snow with two tiny stick limbs poking from both its sides, a bulbous pine cone nose, and two brown eyes made of stones. "He told me!"

Chapter 2

The ensuing weeks did much to loosen the winter's grip on the Derbyshire countryside, as well as bring about a warming in Elizabeth's spirits. She stood outside on the terrace and breathed in the fresh morning air. This was the life she always dreamed she would have: a beautiful home, an adorable child and a wonderful man by her side to help raise him. How she relished this sacred hour of each day before the sun rose to greet the morning sky. This was her time—hers and hers alone. Soon enough, her day would be filled with the hustle and bustle of being the mother of a most precocious young boy, the wife of one of the most prominent men in the county, and the household manager of one of the finest estates in Derbyshire. The addition of Darcy's cousin Anne de Bourgh and his sister, Georgiana, to Elizabeth's family circle increased her joy. And while each day was met with her favourite wish of being with child, for a sister or a brother for Ben would satisfy her fondest wish for familial felicity, as

Elizabeth was not designed for disappointment, she gave a grateful prayer for her many blessings.

As was her wont, Elizabeth quickly made her way down the stone stairs and set out upon the lane. The path she chose that day would carry her past the stable grounds where she might glimpse the horses being attended. Later, she planned to enjoy a brisk morning ride with her husband, but for now she kept walking. Soon, she came to a crossway.

Shall I take the path that leads to the chapel or the one that leads to the temple? A hint of fresh earth in the air recommended she take the latter—that way she might admire all the work being done in the garden in preparation for spring. She had not walked very far before espying another early riser.

"Georgiana, I am surprised to see you out and about so early in the morning," Elizabeth said, as she joined her.

Her manners perfectly unassuming and gentle, Georgiana said, "I will confess that your seeing me is not a coincidence. I wanted to speak with you, away from the house. I surmised this would be the perfect time to garner your undivided attention."

"My dear sister, I know that I have been regularly diverted what with such extensive household responsibilities and the like, but I should hate to suppose I have been neglecting you."

"Oh, no—I do not feel that way at all. In fact, I am more than grateful for all you have done on my behalf."

"Forgive me, but I do not know that I have done anything out of the ordinary."

"I beg to differ. I can well imagine it was no easy feat reining in my brother's grand expectations for me."

"Does this have to do with his desire for you to enjoy your coming out Season this year?"

"Indeed. One would think he were anxious to rid himself of my presence."

"Now, Georgiana, surely you speak in jest. I am certain that the last thing in the world he would want is to *rid* himself of your presence. You must admit he regards himself more as a parent than an older brother. There is nothing so bad as parting with one's child." Elizabeth tried to remain true to her purposes and not be bothered by the fact that her own mother was eager to see all her daughters married, but Georgiana's situation could hardly be compared to that of her three younger sisters who remained at home in Longbourn and whose prospects were not nearly so good. Elizabeth's own marriage to a very wealthy man had done nothing to enhance her younger sisters' lots in life—at least not yet and likely not anytime soon, especially if Georgiana was determined to put off her own coming out for another season.

Elizabeth's own situation told her that her father had done nothing to enhance her three unwed sisters' dowries. Although her own husband was so very rich, he had said nothing of amending her father's lapse and she had certainly never ventured to ask. Through her own economy, she had done what she could to increase her Longbourn family's lot, but, as best she could tell, the funds were put towards more immediate gratifications, such as gowns and bonnets and frivolity and it was never ever enough.

The matter of Georgiana's future was a bone of contention in the Darcy household. True, Darcy was in no hurry to see his sister married and away from Pemberley, but he knew it was his responsibility to see that those very things took place. Georgiana was already eighteen, for heaven's sake. Her thirty thousand pound dowry made her a highly sought after commodity, but it would do no good to delay her destiny just for the sake of his own familial harmony. Elizabeth suspected that a factor in Darcy's readiness to postpone Georgiana's coming out had to do with his desire to see his sister settled with his friend Charles Bingley. This supposition she kept to herself.

Georgiana's aristocratic uncle, Lord Edward Fitzwilliam, the Earl of Matlock, and his wife, Lady Ellen, had their own opinions on the matter, for they were not in favour of any match for their niece that did not have her paired with a young aristocrat or someone else of their own sphere. The same could be said of her aunt Lady Catherine de Bourgh's sentiments. By all appearances, Darcy did not put much stock in his uncle and aunts' preferences. Unfortunately, Georgiana did not seem to put much stock in her uncle's, her aunts', or her brother's preferences.

"Elizabeth, I suppose a Season in town and being presented at court has its advantages, but they certainly are not the prerequisites for happiness as accomplished young women that all would have one believe. You enjoyed neither of those things, and I wager you and my brother are exceedingly happy."

"While it is true that your brother and I find much joy in our marriage, your situation is not to be compared to mine. I was not reared to expect a Season in town, and I was certainly never given to expect a presentation. You, on the other hand, were. How many times have Lady Ellen and Lord Matlock spoken of it as being a favourite wish of your beloved mother, Lady Anne, that you should enjoy all the same benefits that she enjoyed as a young woman? They would view it as a failure to honour her memory to do any less than see you enjoy all the advantages that your family's elevated rank and privilege afford."

"This I understand and it must be said that were I to consent to do so it would only be for the sake of appeasing them—and honouring my mother, of course."

"I continue to have a difficult time comprehending your change in stance as regards your coming out."

"Whatever do you mean?"

"When we met last year, I recall you spoke with such ardent enthusiasm about wanting to come out. What has changed?"

"Truth be told, my eagerness was a mere pretence. Mind you, I had a good reason for speaking as I did. What I dared not say upon first making your acquaintance is I truly do not see that my coming out will help accomplish anyone's purposes, for I am as good as promised to another."

Her brow raised, Elizabeth said, "This is not the first time you have suggested as much, but I do wish you would be more forthcoming with me. Who is this young man to whom you feel you are pledged?"

"Elizabeth, I would love nothing more than to tell you all about him, but I fear that it would place you in an untenable position, for I do not wish to have my brother privy to any of this. You see, he does not approve of the gentleman. If he were aware of my feelings he would be angered, and I have no wish to injure my brother—especially when the entire matter is so tenuous."

"Georgiana, it does not do for you to feel you cannot confide in me. Pray, have you spoken with anyone? Anne perhaps—does Anne know?"

"Heaven forbid!"

"You say that as if your cousin Anne is the last person in whom you would confide."

"Anne and I may have made some progress since she came to live with us here at Pemberley, but I would not say she and I are as intimate as we would have to be before I told her my greatest secrets. Besides, when it comes to such matters, she and my brother are more alike than you would imagine. She surely would not approve of the gentleman either."

"Then I take it that this gentleman, who shall remain unnamed, is known to your family."

"You might say that, although I would say he is not *truly* known, for if they understood his character as I do, then they would surely approve of him."

"Is he someone whom I have met?"

"I do not believe you have met him, but I dare say that, if you had, you would have found him to be charming, amiable, and exceedingly handsome." She folded her hands over her chest. "Oh, Elizabeth, he is everything a gentleman ought to be."

Her eyebrows furrowed, Elizabeth said, "How long has it been since you last saw him?"

"A number of years have passed since I last saw him and, before you ask, no—we do not correspond, for he is too much of a gentleman to dishonour me in that fashion."

"Then, it is safe to say that you do not know what the gentleman's intentions are at present?" Elizabeth read in Georgiana's eyes uncertainty and a lack of enthusiasm that had not been there moments earlier. "Georgiana, I am sorry if my questions give rise to discomfort, but it does not do to hold onto something that might never be, especially as you have determined to delay your coming out and effectively put your life on hold."

"Elizabeth, I am doing what is in my best interest. You see, he is much older than I am—a gentleman of the world, of sense and education. He asked me to wait for him, and I promised him I would. I can do no less."

Chapter 3

Pray my eyes deceive me! Darcy hurried his steps in order to disrupt the disturbing situation unfolding just down the hall. "Mr. Coolidge, Georgiana, pray I am not interrupting."

Slender and soft-spoken, the younger man took a step back. "No, sir, I was just begging Miss Darcy's forgiveness."

Darcy arched his brow. "Pardon?"

Georgiana graced Mr. Coolidge with an angelic smile. "Sir, as I was explaining, there is nothing to forgive."

Darcy said, "Perhaps I should be the judge of that."

"Oh! No, Fitzwilliam. You see, Mr. Coolidge and I nearly collided. I simply was not paying attention to where I was going." She looked at Mr. Coolidge again, her eyes full of sympathy for his awkward plight in being subjected needlessly to her brother's scrutiny. "If the two of you will pardon me, I will be on my way."

Both men watched as Georgiana hurried off. Then Darcy directed his stern gaze at Coolidge, young Ben's tutor.

"Sir, I was on my way to request a private audience with you."

Darcy pursed his lips. This was the last thing he wanted; however, Coolidge was a decent man. The least Darcy could do was grant him this final wish.

"I shall see you in my study."

Moments later, the two men sat on opposite sides of Darcy's large and imposing mahogany desk.

"Sir—" Darcy's guest tugged at his collar. "Mr. Darcy, I wish to speak with you regarding a matter of some importance."

"Certainly, Mr. Coolidge." Oh, how Darcy dreaded the impending discussion. It would certainly not have been the first time a gentleman of meagre means had sought to improve his lot in life by seeking an advantageous alliance. How many times had he seen Coolidge and his sister in situations the uninformed eye would merely interpret as a chance encounter? Then, too, there were those times when Darcy had observed the manner in which Coolidge looked at Georgiana when he thought he was undetected.

Darcy could never recall the tutor being so ill at ease and, although he supposed he would feel decidedly worse once the conversation was over, he sought to make the man feel comfortable. "What is your purpose in requesting this meeting?"

"Well, sir, there is a situation in the class that warrants your attention."

Darcy inwardly exhaled. Coolidge's business had nothing to do with his sister. "So, this meeting has to do with Ben's progress in his studies."

"Indeed, it does, in a manner of speaking. Master Bennet is an exemplary student, and it is such a great pleasure to work with him. What concerns me is his insistence that young Samuel be tutored right alongside him. Frankly, the lad has not the capacity for learning as does the young master. If I am to be completely honest, I would say the situation ends up frustrating us all."

"I was not aware that you were tutoring young Samuel Reynolds right alongside my son. How long has this been going on?"

"It has been going on for the past month, sir."

"I suppose you are acting at Ben's request in an effort to appease him. I know how persistent he can be when it comes to his young friend."

"It is not just Master Bennet who wishes it. Were that only the case, but the situation also enjoys the blessings of his—" The colour washed over Coolidge's face, and he stopped speaking.

"Go on then, Mr. Coolidge. You were about to say."

"Well, sir, I do not wish to speak out of turn, but I fear to say more would risk overstepping my bounds."

Darcy observed the younger man, who appeared far more nervous than he ought to, feverishly searching his brain for the apt words to say. Engaging Coolidge's services had been Mrs. Darcy's idea: a compromise of sorts. Despite his young age, Ben needed the structure of a formal, more advanced education. Darcy had recommended that they consider an elite boarding school until he was old enough to attend Eton. Elizabeth would not hear of being apart from her son at such a young age. It was a matter easily settled, at least for the time being, for Darcy did not truly wish to have Ben away so soon either, even though he posited it was only a matter of time. Ben would indeed be sent to Eton, as had been the case for Darcy and as would be the case for his other, albeit unborn, sons when the time was right.

Mr. Coolidge, the nephew of Darcy's solicitor, was well studied. He had every right to be concerned with the progress he was making with Ben, for if Ben was not benefiting from his tutelage, then he must be away and Ben must be off to boarding school.

"I engaged you primarily for the sake of educating my son. I expect you to be completely forthcoming if there are obstacles in your path that prevent the attainment of the goals we laid out at the start of your employment."

Coolidge shifted his position in the large leather chair. "Perhaps my coming to you in this manner was a mistake, sir. I suppose I might try—"

Darcy stood from his seat and walked around to the other side of his desk to sit opposite the tutor. "What are you trying to avoid telling me?"

"Well, sir, I spoke with Mrs. Darcy, and she is aware of my concerns with having young Samuel present in the schoolroom."

Darcy now understood the young man's predicament for Elizabeth likely dismissed the tutor's concerns in favour of appeasing Ben's wish to have his friend Samuel with him throughout the day.

"You have said enough, sir. For now, I encourage you to do whatever Mrs. Darcy has advised. I will address this matter. Soon you shall find that all of your attention is focused upon Ben's education as it should be. He is advanced in his thinking and reasoning abilities for one who is so young, but that is all the more reason to continue guiding his formal education so that when he is off to boarding school, he will be even further along."

Darcy sent the tutor on his way, and then strode over to the window overlooking a rather well-stocked lake. Ben and Samuel had a habit of fishing there. While Darcy made certain that Ben was well supervised when anywhere near the water, Ben did not necessarily know it. Ben's fierce independent streak would have balked at the very notion of someone watching over him at all times. Ben's friendship with Samuel was not at issue, for Darcy knew how much it meant to his son to have someone of his own age with whom to spend his days. However, Ben needed to understand that he and Samuel were as different as night and day. Ben's future life would be that of a gentleman, a wealthy landowner and master, whereas Samuel, if he worked hard and applied himself, might one day escape the legacy of his birth, that of a servant, and he might become a physician, a lawyer, even a clergyman. He might even be a steward of a large magnificent estate, but he would never be in the same sphere as Ben.

Darcy's mind drifted back to the days of his own youth—days played out in much the same way as Ben was spending his days, whiling away the hours with his closest friend. Darcy's closest friend had been the son of his own father's steward.

George Wickham.

Darcy shook his head. *My beloved father, may his soul rest in peace, never knew what a mistake it had been to expose Wickham to a life that would never be his own—could never be his own.* In fact, Darcy had come to liken his father's charity to a sin: a sin he had no intention of repeating. Darcy could find no fault in young Samuel, none to speak of anyway. He was always polite and good-mannered; just as one would expect of the grandchild of the woman who had been more like a mother to him than a housekeeper in the years after his beloved mother passed away. She was even more so to Darcy's young sister, Georgiana, who never truly knew their mother.

Still, the prospect of putting temptations before young Samuel Reynolds, of planting seeds of want and aspirations of wealth and privilege in the young boy's mind, was something Darcy dared not entertain. He crossed the room with long, determined strides and rang the bell for a footman. *I need to speak with Ben. Now.*

Not long after, Ben and his friend Samuel, to whom Ben attached the appellation Sir Gawain—the most trustworthy friend of Sir Lancelot whenever they took up their Arthurian games, raced into Darcy's study. "Good morning, Da."

"Good morning, Ben." Darcy stood and walked to the boys. "Samuel, how are you this morning?"

"I am getting along very well, sir. I thank you for asking."

Darcy smiled. "You are quite welcome. I should like very much to have a private audience with my son just now."

Ben and Samuel exchanged glances: Ben's questioning and Samuel's contrite.

Turning to his father, Ben said, "Da, I am excited to go riding this morning, and Samuel is too."

"I assure you that what I have to say shall not interfere with your plans. Now run along, Samuel. Ben will join you in the stables as soon as we are done."

Soon after Samuel quitted the room Ben said, "Will you join us on our ride as well? What good fun it would be."

"Not this morning, Ben. Perhaps you and I shall enjoy a ride later this afternoon."

Ben's eyes brightened. "Shall it be the three of us? I should enjoy that even better."

"It will be solely the two of us, Ben."

His shoulders slumped, Ben said, "Da, I cannot help but consider that you are not very fond of Samuel, and I think he feels the same. He was hesitant to come with me for fear you might object to his being here."

"Ben, if your friend was reluctant to enter my study uninvited, then it is as it should be."

"But of course he had an invitation. I invited him."

"So you did."

"Yet you made him feel unwelcome."

How was Darcy to explain to Ben the edicts of etiquette that dictated that servants did not simply gallivant throughout the halls of Pemberley or enter the master's study uninvited? Such behaviour was just the thing that George Wickham would have done when Darcy and he were children. *That turned out very badly.* Fortunately, Ben had never met George Wickham. *To the extent it is within my power, he never will.*

"An unintended consequence, I am sure."

"Then you will reconsider? You will go riding with Samuel and me."

"I never said that."

"Please, Da. I should like that very much."

"You cannot always get what you want."

"I know you tell me that, and I know it is true, but I do not simply want Samuel to share all I enjoy—I rely upon it. It is such a joy to wake each morning knowing we will spend the whole day together."

"Once your lessons are done, you are at leisure to enjoy the entire day with your friend. Indeed, this brings me to my purpose in asking to see you." Darcy took Ben by the hand and encouraged him to have a seat by the fireplace.

"Ben, I need you to understand that your study time is intended solely for you and Mr. Coolidge. I am afraid Samuel's presence comes at your expense. The time Mr. Coolidge is spending with Samuel is time he might otherwise be spending with you."

"What I have found is quite the opposite. You see, I had been spending part of my time teaching Samuel to read and write and add and subtract. I do not agree that it takes time away from my lessons—it adds to my lessons."

"Ben, this really is not a matter for debate."

"Da, why can you not see that this arrangement works out best for all concerned? The time I spend with Samuel on his lessons is time not spent at leisure."

"I suppose the only fallacy in your argument is the premise that you need spend any time at all attending to Samuel's education."

"Oh, but I truly must. Else he will never be able to fully enjoy the tales of the knights of the roundtable on his own. He must continue to rely upon my reading it to him. He would much rather read to himself."

"Ben, did Samuel ask you to take such a task upon yourself?"

Ben cast his eyes downward. "Not in so many words."

"Then how do you know it is important to him?"

"Because! One day, I came across him in the stable poring over the pages of *The Knights of the Roundtable*, struggling to make out the words—with no success whatsoever."

"Your favourite book? How did it come to be in the stables of all places?"

"Well, it used to be my favourite book. It now belongs to Samuel. He told me it is his favourite. But what good is there in having a favourite book if one cannot read a single word it says?"

"I will allow that your reasoning in that regard is sound, and it is a good thing that you wish to see young Samuel establish the same deep appreciation of the legend of King Arthur that you enjoy. However, I will not allow that it is Mr. Coolidge's job to see that it comes about. Samuel is no longer allowed to attend your lessons with you, and you must refrain from encouraging him to do so."

"But, Da?"

"No buts, young man. I believe your friend is waiting for you at the stables. You must not continue to keep him waiting."

Ben remained seated as if refusing to be dismissed so easily as that. How he reminded Darcy of Elizabeth in that regard.

"I should have thought you would have been very proud of my gallantry towards Samuel."

"Ben, I am proud of you."

"Is it not a very noble thing to want to encourage him? Is a proper education not just as important for my friend as it is for me?"

"Your efforts might be described as very noble. However, there are many young children who live amongst the tenants who might benefit equally."

"Then what say you we go about teaching them all?"

"Educating the masses is not something that I have ever given serious consideration, Ben, and for the time being, neither should you. No—my purpose is to do all in my power to see that you are reared as a proper gentleman so that when you reach the age of majority and take your rightful place amongst elite society, you shall be properly prepared."

Elizabeth walked into the room. "Ben, I had not expected to find you here. I thought you and Samuel might be off enjoying some new adventure."

"Mama, I am glad you are here. Da and I cannot agree over a matter that has to do with my friend Samuel and me."

Elizabeth placed her hand on her chest. "What can any of that have to do with me, Ben?"

Darcy said, "I suppose Ben thinks that your opinion of the matter will sway me in my stance."

"Indeed, Mama, you understand why it is so important that Samuel spends time with me in class."

"Perhaps you might give me time alone with your father, young man."

He accepted Elizabeth's proffered embrace, and then walked towards the door. Pausing, he turned and faced Darcy. "Good day, Father."

Good day, Father. How those three innocent words struck Darcy hard as he recalled an agreement he and Ben made, prior to Darcy's and Elizabeth's nuptials, as to how Ben would address him. Ben's words that he would only address him as 'Father' when he was exceedingly vexed echoed in Darcy's ears. Oh, the distress of having disappointed his child for the first time. *The first of many to come, I am sure, although that in no way diminishes my current circumstances. It cannot be helped.*

Once he and Elizabeth were alone, Darcy rubbed his hand across his face. "It is a difficult business being at odds with Ben."

Elizabeth crossed her arms. "Mr. Darcy, unless you can explain your motives you will find yourself at odds with me, as well." She then walked to where he sat and took the seat next to him. "I see no harm in allowing Samuel to join Ben in the schoolroom. In fact, I said as much to Mr. Coolidge. He voiced no objections to the scheme."

He reached out to her, took her hand and cradled it in his. "Elizabeth, my love, I am the one with objections. You will have no way of knowing this, but I have first-hand experience with all that can go wrong when one attempts to lift someone above the sphere in which they were born.

"Indeed, in these very halls of Pemberley did I witness such a travesty unfold. I see in Ben and his friend Samuel a similar situation that I suffered as a young child when my own best friend was the son of my father's steward. It is no wonder that Ben is so fond of Samuel. My childhood friend possessed many of those same admirable qualities that endear young Samuel to everyone he meets. But the fact is that Samuel is the grandson of servants. He is not Ben's equal, and I refuse to regard him as such. I shall not repeat the mistakes of my father."

"So, you truly suppose that allowing Samuel to benefit from the same educational opportunities as Ben equates with regarding him as Ben's equal?"

"I do not intend to take any steps that place me upon the path my father chose. It warms my heart that Ben should have a friend of his own age with whom to spend his days, but I shall not allow Ben to forget that their worlds are leagues apart."

"Will that not be a hard point to argue given that they reside under the same roof?"

"Elizabeth, I do not need to spell out the differences between living above and below stairs to you."

She crossed her arms over her chest and huffed. "I would hope that you do not see fit to *spell it out* for my young son either. I truly do not wish for my son to think of himself as being better than anyone else."

"That does not mean it is not true. Ben is *our* son. He is heir to a fortune of more than two hundred thousand pounds. He will be a wealthy gentleman with expectations of owning a magnificent estate—perhaps even Camberworth, if I can successfully persuade his uncle to sell."

"My, Mr. Darcy, these are lofty goals that you have for our son."

"Have they not always been your goals as well?"

"My greatest goal for Ben just now is that he should enjoy his days of youth. If that means having his friend join him in class, I see no harm."

"What would be next? Shall I see that Samuel owns a horse as fine as Ben's? Shall Samuel be allowed to attend Eton with Ben? Shall he be educated at Cambridge alongside Ben as well?"

"You have asked a series of questions that I am not inclined to address at this point. You know my sentiments as regards boarding school."

"Yes, hence the purpose in Mr. Coolidge's being here, which brings us full circle. My decision is final. Samuel will not be allowed in class with Ben."

"You surprise me, Mr. Darcy. Do you not think it would do Mrs. Reynolds proud to see her grandchild enjoy many of the same privileges as Ben?"

"You will find that Mrs. Reynolds and I are of the same mind in this regard."

"You speak with such confidence. How do you know what her thinking is along those lines? I am rather certain you have not sought her opinion."

"I would have no need to seek her opinion. She, more than anyone, knows the dangers in raising one's expectations beyond what is reasonable for one's sphere. She witnessed first-hand how badly that turned out when my father attempted the same with my childhood friend. She would never wish such a fate for her own flesh and blood. You have never met the rotten fruit of my father's benevolence. Pray you never will."

"Pardon me for thinking it is not sound to conflate your childhood experiences with Ben's." Her voice a mixture of curiosity and frustration, she said, "Who is this childhood friend of whom you speak? Does he have a name?"

"What does it matter to you? He and I have ceased all relationships. He is not welcome to set foot at Pemberley ever again."

"Then it will do no harm if you tell me his name."

Darcy ran his fingers through his hair, and then blew out a long, exasperated breath. "George Wickham."

Chapter 4

Elizabeth was in her sitting room attending to her correspondence when the housekeeper, a respectable-looking, elderly woman, responded to her summons. As Mrs. Reynolds was advancing in years, Elizabeth supposed she would soon be compelled to retire the loyal and faithful servant. It was not something she looked forward to.

"You wished to see me, Mrs. Darcy."

"I did. Thank you for your promptness. Please have a seat, Mrs. Reynolds."

Once the elderly woman took a seat, Elizabeth sat across from her. "May I offer you tea?"

"That is very kind of you, madam, but I must decline."

Elizabeth said, "Very well. I suspect you are anxious to return to your duties. I shall endeavour not to keep you. I wish to discuss the matter of your grandson, Samuel, and Ben. No doubt you are aware of their close camaraderie."

"Oh dear, pray Samuel has not been making a nuisance of himself."

"No, on the contrary, it warms my heart knowing Ben has someone of his own age to while away the long days. This is a first for him, you know. He relies upon his friendship with Samuel, and I can do no less than encourage it." She took a deep breath. "This brings me to the matter I wanted to discuss." Elizabeth knew diplomacy was the order of the day. She did not like to think she was going behind her husband's back, but it was he who had insisted that he and the housekeeper were of one mind on the subject. Elizabeth simply meant to test his conjecture for she could not fathom why anyone would not wish to see one's own kin benefit from a first-rate education.

"What I am about to discuss is a cause for some debate between Mr. Darcy and me. Acting upon Ben's wish to have Samuel join him in class, I asked Mr. Coolidge to factor young Samuel's needs into his lesson plans in addition to Ben's. I see this as a wonderful opportunity for your grandson. However, for reasons that have absolutely nothing to do with Samuel himself and everything to do with a childhood friend of Mr. Darcy's—a Mr. George Wickham—my husband is dead set against the scheme. As I do not know the particulars, Mr. Darcy's strong convictions are hard to countenance. Were he to understand how much it would mean to you to see that young Samuel continues to benefit from Mr. Coolidge's tutelage, I feel strongly that Mr. Darcy would not be opposed to the scheme."

"Mrs. Darcy, pray you will forgive me, but I can see where Mr. Darcy's objections originate. Indeed, it is not unreasonable for him to feel as he does." The housekeeper twisted a linen cloth in her hand. "I know all too well of what he speaks. I do not know how much he told you about his childhood and his being reared alongside him, and I should hate to overstep my bounds by saying more than I ought."

"He has said very little about his childhood friend. In fact, today is the first time I have ever heard his name mentioned. Mr. Darcy posits that his excellent father had done a great disservice in allowing Mr. Wickham to be reared in a manner beyond his sphere."

"As I said, I am no stranger to my late master's generosity. He was George's godfather. Where he meant to see his godson reared as a gentleman with every advantage as well as to give him the means to enjoy a gentleman's life, despite the humble origins of the young man's own parents, George regarded his good fortune as an entitlement. He came to consider himself as equal to the heir of Pemberley, by virtue of the elder Mr. Darcy's benevolence."

"Is that any reason young Samuel should suffer? The situations are not the same."

"Mrs. Darcy, I fear that George Wickham turned out very wild—nothing at all like the fine upstanding young man he portrayed himself to be when the elder Mr. Darcy was alive. I can only attribute it to his realisation and ensuing bitterness that he indeed was never meant to be young Mr. Darcy's equal in consequence—that a generous inheritance did not await him upon his godfather's passing and he would have to rely upon his own devices to attain the manner of living he supposed he ought to have: one befitting a gentleman." Mrs. Reynolds sat up straight and spoke with conviction. "Surely the elder Mr. Darcy would not have treated George Wickham with such favour had he any notion of how the gentleman would turn out.

"Mr. Darcy is an excellent master, and he is every bit as kind and as generous as his father. Everyone who knows him will say the same. If he has misgivings about the prospect of exposing my grandson to the same privileges enjoyed by Master Bennet, who am I to raise objections? I trust the master implicitly, and I am not apt to second guess him, especially where it regards my grandson's well-being. I believe he has been more than generous in allowing Samuel as many liberties as he has already."

"Mrs. Reynolds, you speak with such conviction. Of course, I can do no less than honour your wishes even if I do not agree with them. Young Samuel is such a pleasant lad—so even tempered and good natured. I have never heard a bad thing about him."

"One would imagine, however, that the same was said of a young George Wickham, and, as I said, he turned out very wild. I don't mind saying I would rather no such temptations be placed before my Samuel."

"So, you are content that the lack of a proper education must surely increase his prospects of a life in servitude with no means of escape."

"As long as my grandson is reared with strong guidance and given good examples to follow, I see no harm in that. We all have our own lot in life."

"I did not mean to imply that such a life is less than honourable."

"Indeed, we all have our parts to play. 'Tis the way of the world."

Elizabeth fell silent. She had done her best, but the odds were heavily stacked against her. She had supposed that if Darcy knew how much it meant to Mrs. Reynolds for Samuel to enjoy such an opportunity, she could convince Darcy to go along with the scheme. Alas, it was not to be. Both Mr. Darcy and Mrs. Reynolds were determined not to repeat what they viewed in hindsight as a mistake on the elder Mr. Darcy's part as regarded his godson—the son of his own steward.

What would be the point in arguing with them both, especially as she was loath to relinquish such decisions when it came to her own son? *The question is: How shall I help Ben understand?*

Mrs. Reynolds said, "I suspect this is not what you wanted to hear, Mrs. Darcy. It is the way it must be. I have never done anything other than my master's bidding, and nothing anyone can say or do will ever change that." She stood and smoothed her skirt. "I beg your pardon, madam. I must return to my duties."

Elizabeth's ensuing discomfort of the elderly woman's attitude would hardly be repressed. She seemed to take Elizabeth's good intentions as an effrontery. *This shall only complicate matters as regards our relationship, I suppose.*

I cannot say I blame her—not entirely. Till this day, any mention of sending Ben away to boarding school riled her. It was too soon. He was too young. Should Mr. Coolidge remain in their employ for the next decade, it would suit Elizabeth just fine. Of course, Mr. Darcy would never hear of it. *It is as though he has every hour of Ben's life planned.*

Elizabeth drifted to the window and folded her arms over her bosom as she stared outside. *I know he only has Ben's best interest at heart and only wants what is best for Ben.* Elizabeth was just unaccustomed to relinquishing control over Ben's life. For so long she had been the only one making decisions for Ben, and now Mr. Darcy had effectively relieved her of that distinction. What a bittersweet conundrum she faced: being married to the best man in the world and having him shoulder her every burden, when anything having to do with her son she did not consider a burden at all. Being Ben's mother had defined her every waking moment for so long.

Ceding control to another is not going to be easy.

Chapter 5

The time had come for the Darcys to take their annual leave of Pemberley. Although Georgiana would not be coming out, being in London was the thing to do. Darcy had always been in town during the Season. This year, he especially looked forward to being there with his bride. But first there was the obligatory springtime journey to Kent to visit Lady Catherine de Bourgh. How different this visit would be. For the first time in more years than Darcy cared to recall, his aunt would not be determined to force him to propose to his cousin. Matters had gotten so far out of hand that Darcy threatened his aunt with never visiting her again if she did not desist in her matchmaking scheme. The prospect of falling out of favour with a most beloved nephew had been sufficient to silence her on the matter forever.

Elizabeth, Georgiana, and even Anne anticipated the upcoming trip with delight. If only the same could be said of young Ben. Leaving Pemberley was the last thing he wanted.

London was a horrible place, he often complained. Nothing good ever happened in London, whereas his days at Pemberley were amongst the happiest days in his life.

It would be summer time before the Darcys returned to Derbyshire, yet another fact that did not sit well with Ben, for it meant being parted from Samuel. The two boys were nearly inseparable—that is, once Ben had completed his daily lessons. As the days leading up to the Darcys' leave-taking drew nearer, Ben grew increasingly uncharacteristically quiet. This change did not escape Darcy's notice. Indeed, it troubled him exceedingly, for he was certain that visiting Rosings Park, which Ben affectionately referred to as Camelot, would stir Ben's hopes for a repeat of their many fun adventures.

On the eve of their trip, Darcy visited Ben in his room to wish him a good night's rest.

"Ben, are you as excited as I am over the prospect of visiting Camelot once more?"

"I suppose I am."

"You are doing an excellent job of hiding your enthusiasm, young sir. Pray, what is the matter?"

"You must know how much I looked forward to having Samuel come with us."

"I understand how disappointed you are."

"You know that Samuel will be off to visit his other grandparents for the summer. Who is to say we shall ever see each other again? Oh, please reconsider and allow him to accompany us on our journey. I have told him all about Camelot and what great fun we had."

"Ben, you and I have talked about this before, have we not? The possibility of Samuel's travelling with us is nonexistent."

"But I shall have a pause from my studies," Ben protested.

"There is a larger matter at stake. It has to do with issues I fear you are far too young to comprehend."

Ben frowned. "What sort of issues, Da?"

Darcy tucked in Ben's covers. "This is a discussion for when you are older, son."

"Not too much older, I hope."

Darcy placed a light kiss atop Ben's head. "Get plenty of rest. We shall have an early start tomorrow." After blowing out the bedside candle, Darcy walked outside the door. He paused a moment, in deep reflection. Were he inclined to grant Ben his favourite wish—which Darcy most certainly was not—the outcome would prove disastrous. Oh, how his aunt Lady Catherine would react were young Samuel to arrive in Kent with them! The one time his father had brought George Wickham to Kent was forever impressed upon Darcy's mind, despite the passage of nearly two decades. Her outrage had been palpable; her protests, unrestrained. She had been correct in her strong objections to George Darcy's preferential treatment of the son of his steward, and what was worse, everything that she had predicted about how badly it would end up had come to pass.

Darcy frowned. Finding his thinking aligned with his aunt's was troubling indeed, but such was the case—regardless of whether he liked it or not. He would be damned if he repeated his father's greatest mistake.

Elizabeth's dearest Aunt and Uncle Gardiner had been unable to travel to Derbyshire at Christmastime. Hence, it was important for Elizabeth to spend whatever time she could with them before she and her family journeyed to Kent for Easter. The Gardiners had invited the Darcys to have dinner in Cheapside. As the scheme allowed Ben to enjoy his younger cousins' company, everyone easily conceded.

After dinner, while Mr. Gardner and Darcy enjoyed port, Elizabeth and her aunt discussed those things that mattered most to members of the fairer sex. "From your letters, I would say things turned out far better than expected, considering the circumstances," said Mrs. Gardiner, an amiable, intelligent, elegant woman, and a great favourite with all her nieces.

"Yes, well, if you are referring to my husband and Geoffrey Collins, I am happy to say the two showed a willingness to pretend to get along. Whether their seeming accord will be of a long lasting duration remains to be seen."

"Actually, I was thinking more of your own accord with your sister Jane as well as with your father."

"I did write speaking of the cordiality between us all."

"Yes, but I dare say there are some things more easily confided in person."

"This is true. You are no stranger to my strong convictions against the alliance between my dearest sister and the man who would be my worst enemy, but I have come to consider my concerns were born out of my dislike of Geoffrey Collins for the harsh way he treated Ben and the manner in which he came to regard me.

"The reality is that there was some truth in his deep distrust of my relationship with Fitzwilliam. He made no secret of his feelings towards me even though I was *engaged* to Geoffrey Collins. In hindsight, I might have done more to discourage him." Elizabeth smoothed her skirt. "The truth is I did not discourage Fitzwilliam. In fact, I enjoyed the attention he bestowed. I longed for it."

"Then, it is indeed better that you and Geoffrey Collins parted company."

"Indeed. As for Jane, she seems very content with her lot in life. She adores the twins, Gillian and Emily." Elizabeth smiled in fond remembrance of the lovely young ladies. "Who could not? If I have any regrets, they are born of my own disappointed hopes that plans for our future felicity with me as their mother fell apart. However, Jane is an excellent mother and I daresay she loves Geoffrey Collins as well."

"All is well that ends well," said Elizabeth.

Mrs. Gardiner commenced preparing tea. She handed a cup to her niece. "And what say you of your relationship with your father? Have the two of you put all of your differences aside?"

"I would say he and I have made great strides in that regard. We no longer suffer contention over my going against his wishes and marrying Ben's father. It pleases me immensely that he showed such interest in Ben. Family means so much to my darling son. Papa and he grew very close during their time at Pemberley."

"I suppose Ben was saddened upon learning he would not be spending time with his grandfather during the trip from Pemberley owing to my brother Bennet's being in Lincolnshire visiting Jane, along with the rest of the family."

"This is true. However, there is the promise of reuniting the two of them in due time. We journey to Derbyshire at the end of the Season."

"Then you certainly do plan on enjoying your first Season as Mrs. Darcy here in town."

"I shall do my best. First, I must survive my first visit as Mrs. Darcy in Kent. I should imagine everything will be a small matter, by comparison."

"From the stories you have told me about Lady Catherine, I can well imagine."

"Fortunately, her ladyship shows a great affinity for Ben, owing to her close friendship with Ben's grandmother."

"You are speaking of the late Mrs. Sarah Carlton."

"Indeed. What is more, her ladyship rather enjoys the company of Geoffrey Collins, so much so that she strongly suggested that he, Jane, and the girls are to stay at Rosings when next they visit."

"Will wonders never cease?"

"Indeed. If Lady Catherine has her way, I would not be surprised if the Collinses visit Kent as soon as my father, my mother, and my younger sisters take their leave from Lincolnshire." Elizabeth took a measured sip from her cup of tea. "What a gay reunion that will be."

Matters between Darcy and Mr. Gardiner were not as agreeable. Darcy owed it to his having relieved Mr. Gardiner of his role as trustee of Elizabeth's financial holdings soon after the wedding. The things Elizabeth had confided in him about her uncle's handling of her finances had done nothing to recommend him to Darcy. If anything, it had served quite the opposite effect. Darcy had no tolerance for speculation. However, he could not object to Mr. Gardiner in his entirety, for by Elizabeth's account her uncle had been more of a father to her than Mr. Bennet had been, not only in negotiating the marriage settlement to her first husband—such as it was—but also in escorting her down the aisle. For that reason alone, Mr. Gardiner had earned his niece's eternal gratitude, and no amount of financial mismanagement of her funds would alter that. Darcy would endeavour to honour him no less.

Mr. Gardiner, a sensible, gentlemanlike man, and as best Darcy could tell, greatly superior to his sister, as much by nature as education, cleared his throat. "So, you very well intend to procure the Carlton family estate for young Ben. I was always of the opinion my niece wanted nothing to do with any of that."

"Where matters of finances are concerned, I follow my own counsel."

"I mean no offence; it is just that Lizzy's goals for Ben have not always aligned with your current agenda."

My agenda! This is the opinion of the man who has been the means of decimating the bulk of Elizabeth's financial holdings. Indeed, the older man's attitude bothered Darcy more than a little. "Sir, with all due respect, I appreciate your concerns, but I will act in a manner that constitutes my wife's and my son's best interests."

Chapter 6

Soon upon entering the park, Elizabeth's chest tightened. Feelings she thought she had long ago left behind made their presence known as a result of her returning to the place that had borne witness to one of the most angst-ridden chapters of her life.

She had spent a month at the parsonage as a guest of her sycophant cousin, Mr. William Collins, and his wife, Charlotte, along with the man who would have been her husband had her father and the gentleman himself had their way. Elizabeth's realisation that she would never be happy with such a man and that she surely was incapable of making him happy was met with bitterness and harsh accusations when she told him as much. She would have been helpless had her friend Charlotte not advanced her the funds to travel to London after the bitter parting of the ways with Mr. Geoffrey Collins who had made it clear that he never wished to lay eyes on her again. *Indeed, so much has changed. Geoffrey Collins is my brother, married to my dearest sister, Jane.*

What a terrible period it had been indeed. However, her time in Kent had not been entirely bad. She had spent many pleasurable hours in Mr. Darcy's company. The passing scenery outside her window evoked rousingly pleasing sentimentalities as the carriage drove past the lane that would forever be known as her favourite in Rosings Park, for it was on that lane that he had professed his undying love for her and offered her his hand in marriage. *The spot just over there by the tree is where I first tasted his lips.*

Although married for many months, the thought of being in his arms and of being kissed by him for the very first time unleashed a swarm of butterflies in her stomach.

Darcy who had been rather subdued since their initial greeting that morning had caught Elizabeth wholly unawares with the intensity of his plea.

"In vain, I have struggled not to act upon our undeniable attraction to one another, but rather to allow us to become better acquainted without crossing the boundaries of your ill-judged arrangement with your cousin. It will not do.

"It was all I could do not to take you and Ben by the hand and lead you from the church yesterday. It is increasingly heart wrenching to see just how miserable Ben is under the gentleman's tutelage. It is equally tormenting to witness your suffering, as well."

Darcy moved nearer to Elizabeth and took her into his arms, as though it were the most natural thing in the world. "I want you, Elizabeth, with every fibre of my being. I want you. You and I belong together. I long to be by your side. I want you to be mine."

His lips met hers for the very first time. Warm, moist, and inviting, his kiss was all she had dreamed it would be and more. Darcy ceased his amorous attentions to her lips.

"Please, forgive me—for my trespass against you. I had no right. I can offer no excuse other than to confess you mean the world to me. There is not a day that goes by that I do not wish to be with you. I want you in my life; please say you will share the rest of your days with me."

The abrupt cessation of his lips on hers brought Elizabeth around to her right mind, as well. Enveloped in his arms felt wonderfully fitting. Yet, how could it be? Fighting against her body's own aching desire and her lonely heart's ardent pleading, she pulled herself from his gentle embrace, turned, and walked a few steps away.

Far too many months had passed before she found herself similarly captured in his loving embrace, despite the fact that she and Ben came to reside at Pemberley, under Darcy's protection, owing to life's disastrous turn of events. It was the night of his second proposal. Elizabeth's mind meandered tenderly to that magical time.

The stars were shining brighter than she ever recalled. The two of them stood on the balcony. Lost in the moment, Elizabeth remained silent throughout as she nestled in his arms. She could not imagine anything more thrilling; the sheer delight of his arm freely resting along her waist, the warmth of his breath tracing softly along her neck, and his hands gently touching hers. It was such a pleasure for Elizabeth to be ensconced in Darcy's embrace. She relished the intoxicating effects of the excitement engendered by his tender, arousing voice. Then, Darcy unhurriedly relinquished his impassioned hold, though he did not let go of her hand.

"Elizabeth, I have but one wish to voice before we part for the evening ... surely you must know what it is. My great-

est wish is that you will marry me, that I shall soon be a husband to you and a father to Ben. Please do me the honour of accepting my hand."

Reminiscences of the adoration that shone on his face when she whispered, "Wish granted," gently nudged her to the present. In spite of indulging herself in reflection that was best reserved for solitary hours, Elizabeth smiled in anticipation of what the next three weeks in Kent entailed. How different it would be visiting Rosings as a member of the family as opposed to the object of fascination to relieve Darcy's aunt Lady Catherine de Bourgh's curiosity.

Elizabeth supposed Darcy's cousin Anne, who now resided with them at Pemberley, was just as anxious at being in Kent once again. When Lady Catherine had visited them in Derbyshire over Christmas, she made no secret of her desire to have Anne return to Kent where she truly belonged. Having reconciled herself to the Darcys' marriage, her ladyship was intent upon making another alliance for Anne—ideally, someone that she had handpicked.

"Anne, you have been very quiet since we entered the park."

"I am merely taking the time to enjoy the calm before the storm."

"Surely it will not be so bad as that. Lady Catherine was on her best behaviour at Christmas."

"Indeed, that is what worries me. It is not like my mother. I fear she was merely biding her time. Now that I am once again in Kent, she likely will stop at nothing in seeing that I remain here."

"Rosings Park is a magnificent estate and it *will* be yours one day. I would think you would want to be here," said Georgiana, as if her sentiments on the matter were not already known. She and Anne had made some strides, but

Elizabeth supposed even a lifetime of felicity would not erase years of bad blood between the cousins. Elizabeth recalled her husband say that his good opinion once lost was lost forever. She could well imagine that being Georgiana's mantra as well.

"I declare, dear cousin, you are more like my mother than you are aware. Have you forgotten I am a guest at your brother's and Elizabeth's home—the same as you? We both are the happy recipients of their benevolence."

"I believe my right to be at Pemberley is inherent in my birth, just as it is your birthright to reside in Kent."

"I will not argue with you, but it must be said that, as regards being at Pemberley, you and I are on equal footing. We are both merely guests. Once you have fulfilled your legacy of securing a husband, you will discover that on your own. My advice to you is to choose your husband wisely—a dowry of thirty thousand pounds is not much to boast about unless your husband is a man of some consideration in the world, whereas I might choose to marry anywhere I wish, and my prospects will not be diminished one bit."

Georgiana shifted restlessly in her seat. She coloured. She said nothing in reply, giving Elizabeth cause to wonder. Her sister had spoken of being promised to another, although she had been rather vague in her description of the gentleman, and try as Elizabeth might to find out the gentleman's name, Georgiana had kept that information to herself.

Surely he is a gentleman with the means of providing for Georgiana in a manner suitable to the only sister of one of the wealthiest gentlemen in Derbyshire. Elizabeth knew and understood her husband's hopes for his sister well enough to know he would countenance nothing less.

The carriage rounded the curve, and there it stood—the sun beaming off the glazing, Rosings was indeed a sight to behold. Elizabeth recalled Ben's first time seeing the magnificent place as well as his wide-eyed enthusiasm over its being Camelot. As for herself, never had Elizabeth been so happy to see the manor house, for it meant a cessation of the cousins' bickering—if only for a short while.

Darcy was quick to reach the carriage so he might have the pleasure of handing his lovely wife from the carriage himself. The last leg of the journey had seemed longer than ever before as his mind raced ahead to the pleasures that awaited him once he and Elizabeth were in the manor house and settled comfortably in their rooms. How different this trip to Kent would be over the last. The last was marked by countless nights of loneliness and painful, unsatisfied longings. Now each night would be spent with his wife in his arms.

After handing Elizabeth from the carriage, it did not take long to see that something was amiss. Georgiana and Anne did not appear very pleased to be there. He looked at his wife. "How did you find the last part of the trip, my love?"

"The carriage ride was comfortable enough, although I cannot say the trip was wholly uneventful." She threw a glance towards Georgiana and then Anne.

His voice low, his warm breath caressed her ear. "Are the two of them once again at odds?"

"Is there even a need to ask? What say we put off this discussion for another time?" Ben raced up to his mother, took her by the hand, and started coaxing her along. Darcy smiled at the young lad's enthusiasm. As soon as they had entered the park, Ben's excitement took hold. He had spoken of little else other than the prospect of being once again in Camelot and all the fun that was to be had within its environs.

Darcy headed over to his sister's side with the intention of lightening her spirits. He knew her well enough to know the one thing she wanted most from the trip was for it to end with Anne's being left behind.

Having always prided himself on his determination to do whatever it took to bring a smile to her face, the one place he had drawn the line was in regards to their cousin Anne. Georgiana was most unhappy with his decision to have Anne live with them at Pemberley for as long as she wished. His sister did not trust their cousin; she even complained of Darcy's unwavering impartiality to his cousin, and she blamed Anne for making Darcy's life miserable for so many years with her deathbed schemes.

He had lost count of the number of times her ladyship had summoned him to Rosings Park on the excuse that Anne desperately needed him else all hope was lost. Finally he had enough—he declared his intention never to set foot at Rosings again should Anne and his aunt persist in their hopeless quest. Nevertheless, his familial affection for Anne did not wane and once she had suffered and subsequently recovered from a true near death experience, a heartfelt apology on her part was all it had taken—one proffered to both Elizabeth and to him—to earn Anne a place in their new family, much to Georgiana's chagrin.

How disappointed he had been that Georgiana had put off her coming out Season that year. Even though he was not anxious for her to make her debut in Society and toss her hat into the marriage market as it were, still it must be done. His suspicion that his young sister was enamoured of Ben's tutor, Mr. Coolidge, had not waned. *Surely she must know I would never countenance such an alliance. Why, the gentleman is so far beneath Georgiana in consequence as to be laughable.* On the other hand, Darcy could scarcely deny that an alliance between his sister and his friend Charles Bingley would meet with no objections—at least not from him. His aristocratic uncle and aunts might have something to say; however, their opinions would not influence him so long as such an alliance was something Georgiana truly desired.

Then again, it is entirely likely that Bingley has met and fallen in love with someone else. The last he had heard from Bingley, he was hopelessly in love with a woman who had committed herself to another—said woman being his own sister Jane. Though Darcy had never detected any symptoms of love in Jane towards Bingley, he had to allow that his friend's feelings for her were as strong as ever. As difficult a time as he had in deciphering Bingley's hastily-written, barely-legible letters, the message that sprang from the pages was the repeated references to the former Miss Bennet.

* * *

Lady Catherine was glad for her daughter's return as evidenced by her warmer than usual greeting when all her guests arrived, as well as her cheery demeanour at dinner. "How do you get along at Pemberley, my dear?" Lady Catherine said to her daughter.

"I find it absolutely delightful, Mother. Thank you for asking."

A tall, large woman, with strongly marked features, which might once have been handsome, Lady Catherine acknowledged her daughter with a slight nod, before continuing her inquisition. "And your health? Are you making certain to take care so there are no relapses of the malady that often afflicted you while you were here?"

"I am happy to say I have suffered no such relapses."

"Very well. I should like to suppose that you are home to stay."

"Mother, I am glad to be here, but I have not resolved on staying or leaving at this point. We shall see."

Anne looked at Darcy and Elizabeth, hoping to see some sign of how they regarded her lack of decision, but she saw nothing that attested to their sentiments. Georgiana's face brightened— the same as it always did when she thought Anne would be taking her leave. What was most important to Anne, however, was the prospect of seeing her cousin Richard again. She knew she would always see him as long as she resided at Pemberley. However, the only time she would ever see him again should she decide to remain at Rosings was at Easter. Anne truly did liken her time at Rosings to more of a prison sentence. Never did she and her mother go anywhere or do anything that did not serve as the means of satisfying her mother's desires, whether it was travelling to town or to the coast.

If her mother truly did miss her company, it was because she was simply tired of rattling around in that big empty mausoleum by herself.

Colonel Richard Fitzwilliam arrived late that evening after most of the household had retired. He did, however, have word sent to Darcy of his safe arrival as well as his desire for an early-morning ride—that was, if his cousin could manage to tear himself away from his dear wife.

Darcy and Richard had just finished a strenuous horseback race. Now they guided their horses along at a leisurely pace.

Darcy spoke first. "I was beginning to suspect you might not join us here at Rosings this year, my friend."

"I am not one to eschew family traditions out of hand, although in this case I was sorely tempted. As you are no doubt aware, Father is intent upon an alliance between Anne and me. Making matters worse, the last time I saw Lady Catherine at Pemberley over Christmas, I saw that look in her eyes."

"That look?"

"Do not feign ignorance, Darcy. You know of what I speak. I saw the same look bestowed upon you every year since you reached the age of majority now directed towards me."

"Oh, *that* look." Darcy shrugged. "Would marrying Anne be the worst thing in the world? You are getting no younger, you know, and marriage to Anne would be the means of keeping you in the manner of living befitting the second son of an earl."

"Have you been speaking with Lord Matlock, too?"

"I am only speaking the truth, my friend."

"Of course, were Anne to marry, she would no longer be living at Pemberley. Is that part of the reason you are trying to persuade me to marry her?"

"On the contrary. I would not wish to see the two of you married merely for my own convenience. I would only wish it were it something both of you desired."

"Then, you are not finding it inconvenient having Anne live with you at Pemberley?"

"You know how important Anne is to me. I would not object to her living with us always. Georgiana—on the other hand…"

Richard laughed knowingly. "So, all is not tranquil in paradise."

"Where I had once held hope they would put their differences aside, I fear it is not to be. The more time they spend together, the more they continue to grow at odds. I fear Georgiana is not of a mind to forgive Anne."

"That should not be of concern much longer. Surely Georgiana is planning to meet and marry a lucky gentleman in the near future."

"Indeed, he would be a lucky man. However, I do not believe my sister is the least bit interested in the prospect." By now, Darcy and Richard had arrived at the stables, and they charged the groom with their horses. Darcy said, "I cannot fault her in not wishing to change things. For the first time in a long time, Pemberley is more than just a house or a grand estate; it is a home. She and Elizabeth are as close as two sisters ought to be, and she absolutely adores being Ben's aunt. I do not know that I have ever seen my sister so happy as she is now. Still, I want her to partake in the Season. I am aware your mother is most anxious to oversee her coming out and her presentation at court."

"True, Mother was quite looking forward to this being Georgiana's first Season."

"I will insist upon next Season."

"No more excuses, aye?"

"Indeed. No more excuses."

"Speaking of excuses, whatever happened to your notion of an alliance between your friend Charles Bingley and Georgiana?"

Darcy looked at Richard intently. "That was—rather *is*—a favourite wish of mine, but I will never be accused of playing matchmaker. Should there ever be anything of a tender regard between my friend Bingley and my sister, I would rather prefer that it unfolded naturally."

"It is interesting you say that."

"Why do you say such a thing, Richard? What is so interesting about my stance?"

"I seem to recall you saying you had saved your friend from an unhappy alliance some time back, owing to the unsuitability of the lady's family. I rather supposed your motives were tied to your hopes for Georgiana."

Darcy coloured. "For heaven sakes, man. If you insist upon bringing up events from the past, you might as well recall them correctly. While it is true that my desire to leave Hertfordshire rather precipitously may have been the means of Bingley being parted from the young woman in question, I did not force him to do it. He might have stayed and pursued Jane had he wished it."

Richard tugged at the reins of his horse. "Jane! How could I have missed the connection all this time? So, Jane was the young woman whose family you found so objectionable? Does Elizabeth know any of this?"

"If you are asking me if my wife knows that I found her family objectionable at one time, I see no reason she could not have known. It is not as though I made a secret of how I felt about them. I was struck by her beauty—her liveliness from the moment I first laid eyes on her. As for Elizabeth, that she was connected to the Bennets was not even something that I had allowed as a possibility. Having spent time with them at Pemberley, you can have no doubt of what I speak. My feelings for Elizabeth were so strong as to overlook any inadequacies in her family."

"True, your wife has little in common with her family, to be sure, other than familial resemblance, but the same must be said of Jane. I can see why your friend Bingley was taken with her. She is divine, she is indeed an angel."

"Let us not forget that she is married."

"Indeed, and what a shame that is."

"I do not know that one can describe Jane's situation in those terms. I daresay she is very contented with her situation."

"Oh! I would not venture to say otherwise as regards her marital felicity. When I spoke of what a shame it is, I believe I thought only of myself."

Chapter 7

To Elizabeth's way of thinking, one of the best things about being in Kent was the prospect of spending time with her intimate friend Charlotte. Elizabeth could not wait a moment longer in bringing the reunion about, and so she set off early that morning on the path leading to the parsonage. Charlotte greeted Elizabeth at the gate, and the two ladies embraced with all the warmth befitting friends separated by hundreds of miles.

When they were settled in Charlotte's particular parlour, Elizabeth reached for her friend's hand and gave it a good squeeze. "Charlotte, it is such a pleasure to see you again. It is all well and good to keep in touch through letters, but it is a poor substitute for actually being together like this."

"It was so very nice seeing you at Pemberley over Christmas, dearest Eliza."

"Indeed. Who would have thought that we all should be reunited at Pemberley after the manner of my leave-taking when I was a guest here at the Parsonage?"

"Yes, but that is all behind us now, or so I would like to think. You and my brother Geoffrey got along swimmingly, though one would never venture to say that he and your husband shall ever enjoy the kind of camaraderie two brothers ought; however, that the two of them were civil was a refreshing change."

"I confess you are correct, although I did not always expect them ever to get along. You will recall the level of animosity between those two when we were all here last spring."

"I suppose that is the way it is when two strong and determined gentlemen have their caps for the same woman. In the end, things turned out just as they ought. Jane seemed very much in love with Geoffrey, and Mr. Darcy is very much in love with you. You deserve every bit of the happiness you enjoy with your husband."

Some discussion was had over Elizabeth's familial felicity and how she often found herself caught in the middle of disagreements between Georgiana and Anne and, at times, Ben and Darcy.

Charlotte said, "I am sure you would not have it any other way."

"Indeed, only you would say such a thing, dear Charlotte."

"Who knows you better than I do—save Jane and your dear husband … perhaps?"

Elizabeth said, "Indeed, I would say that my husband and I are well on our way to knowing each other perfectly, which is not to say we do not have our fair share of disagreements, for there is one thing I first only suspected about my dear husband that I now know without a doubt to be true."

"Pray what is that, dear Eliza, if you do not mind my asking?"

"He likes to have his own way."

Charlotte laughed at this revelation. "That should hardly come as a surprise. Is that not the way with rich and powerful men?"

Frantic tapping against the window pane drew the ladies' eyes towards the direction of the sound. Charlotte excused herself and crossed the room in haste. She opened the window. Her husband looked as if he had been dragged there by his horse.

Panting, he said, "Wait until you hear what I have rushed all this way to say."

"My dear Mr. Collins, you must calm yourself."

After a series of shallow breaths, his hand clutching his chest, he said, "Do not make yourself uneasy, my dear, but I have just come from Rosings Park."

She placed her hand on her bosom. "Oh!"

"Indeed. It seems the arrival of the Darcys has pleased my noble patroness exceedingly, and she is once again of a mind to entertain guests."

Charlotte could well imagine how happy this made her husband, for it had been months since her ladyship invited them to tea, much less dinner. After church services, she regularly lamented on the pain she must suffer having to be alone away from her dear Anne. It was too much to endure and yet endure it she would. Until her Anne returned, she would not even consider entertaining anyone at Rosings. Such was her refrain whenever she was seen in public—she would bear her lot alone and in silence.

Collins said, "Her ladyship is delighted to have her daughter home again where she belongs, and she is being exceedingly generous towards the Darcys too, in spite of their encouraging Miss de Bourgh to be away from her mother at a time in life when her ladyship needs her only child most. I do not know that I would be quite so generous."

"My dear Mr. Collins, please greet our guest."

The ridiculous man's mouth gaped. His eyes widened. "Our guest? Why did you not say something before?" He poked his head inside and espied Elizabeth sitting on the couch, thus obliging Elizabeth to join her friend at the window.

"My dear cousin, I had no idea you were here. Welcome to our humble abode. I do hope everything is to your liking."

"Indeed, it is, sir."

"I beg your pardon for what I said just now. It is a most Christian act to open your home to Miss de Bourgh. As I recall, she is most happy there, although you likely heard me express my happiness on her ladyship's behalf to know that her daughter is returned."

"Indeed, sir, and whether Anne decides to remain here in Kent upon our leave-taking is not for me to say, but I assure you, my husband and I will be agreeable as well as accommodating to whatever she decides, even if that means once again being the means of keeping her from being here with Lady Catherine at a time when her mother desperately needs her most."

* * *

Days later, Anne woke up earlier than had been her wont the

last time she stayed in that room—her room, the room in which she had passed the bulk of her youth. It was not unlike her room at Pemberley with its large canopied bed with navy satin covers. Albeit not very feminine, as Lady Catherine often complained, navy blue was Anne's favourite colour; hence, it was settled that her room should be of said colour.

There was a special reason for her early awakening. She planned to have breakfast with her cousin Richard and, if she were persuasive enough, she would encourage him to have a turn around the garden afterwards. Anne liked her cousin very much and should she find herself the happy recipient of his tender regard, then she would not complain. Of course, she needed to be careful to be subtle in her attempts to garner his affections. After the manner of her wild and out of control pursuit of Darcy, Anne never wished to make such a mistake again. In this attempt, she had her uncle Matlock's blessing.

Or maybe it was not such a blessing after all, for he had been the one to persuade me to pursue Darcy as zealously as I did. What a mistake that had been. Anne did not intend to make the same mistake twice. Her hand on the door handle, she released it and headed back to her dressing table. Her maid had done a fine job with her hair. In addition, Anne's manner of dress had improved considerably of late. She ran her hands along her face. *I can surely stand a bit more colour.* With that, she pinched her cheeks. *Oh, what is the use? No—I must not think that way. If I am to garner my cousin's affections, I must be positive.*

Anne was sitting at the table when Richard sauntered into the room. "Anne, what a surprise it is to see you this morning."

"Not an unwelcome surprise, I hope."

Richard walked over to the sideboard and loaded his plate with eggs and assorted meats.

"Quite the contrary. It is always a pleasure to have someone to dine with. Normally that would have been Darcy, but I suppose his newfound marital felicity renders him a late riser."

Richard remembered that, in spite of his cousin's age and her near-spinster status, she likely retained the sensibilities of a maiden. He coloured. "I beg your pardon, Anne."

"You need not apologise. Even young Ben has made mention of his parents' wont of being late risers, unlike before they were married."

Richard smiled heartily at this account of his young cousin. "Anne, how are you enjoying your stay at Pemberley?"

"I can honestly say I am spending some of the happiest days of my life."

"I am delighted to hear that. It is just as I knew it would be."

"Yes, you were very instrumental in helping me to face the reality of my situation. I do declare I find myself forever in your debt—one I am most eager to settle."

"Your happiness is all the repayment I could ever want."

"You are very kind to me, Richard. And though we have not always seen eye to eye, I should like to say that you and I are well on our way to being the dearest of cousins as well as friends."

*If my father had his say, we would be much more than friend*s. He dare not say a word of that to Anne. He knew not how she might feel, but it would not do to give her false hope. As much as he was beginning to appreciate his cousin, he did not suffer the kind of attraction that might render him a suitable husband for her, regardless of his father's hopes and dreams.

* * *

"Elizabeth, I received word that you wanted to see me." Darcy espied his wife sitting in the window seat overlooking the gardens where Ben was playing outside. She clutched a letter. He hurried to her side. "Elizabeth, you have been crying." He brushed her tears from her cheek. "What has happened?"

"I have a letter from Jane."

"Has something happened to one of her family?"

"Jane writes from Longbourn. Papa has suffered a stroke, at least that is what Jane suspects. He is rendered incapacitated, barely conscious and unable to speak. I am afraid the news is very grim."

"Elizabeth, my love, I am truly sorry. I trust you will want to leave Kent and travel to Hertfordshire."

"Yes, as soon as can be."

Darcy leaned forward and encouraged her into his strong embrace. "Of course, as soon as can be. I shall make arrangements." He stood and took her by the hand. "Come. Lie here and rest while I see to our departure."

Moments later, Darcy found his cousin lounging in the parlour. "Richard, Elizabeth has received grave news from Hertfordshire. It has to do with her father. I am afraid he may have suffered a stroke."

"That is grave indeed."

"You will understand that Elizabeth is most anxious to take her leave of Kent so she might be by her father's side. It dictates that she and I travel light and with all due haste. I shall need a favour of you."

"Anything, my friend. You need only ask, and I will do all I can."

"I was counting on you to say that. I ask you to see that Georgiana and Ben are escorted to London. You may take them to stay with Lord and Lady Matlock until Elizabeth and I fully discern the situation in Hertfordshire."

Relying heavily upon the aid of her walking stick, Lady Catherine ambled into the room. "What is it that you are saying about a situation in Hertfordshire, Darcy?"

"Elizabeth has received word from Longbourn of a rather sad nature as regards her father."

"Pray he is not dead. This must certainly affect the fortune of Mr. Collins's eldest brother whom I recall as being the heir."

Both Darcy and Colonel Fitzwilliam spoke in unison, "Lady Catherine!"

"You need not feign such outrage, nephews. People die."

Darcy rolled his eyes and whispered a silent prayer of thanksgiving that his wife was not there to bear witness to his aunt's callousness. "For heaven's sake, Lady Catherine, guard your tongue. Mr. Bennet lives; however, he has suffered a stroke and the prognosis is dire. I was asking Richard if he would see that Georgiana and Ben arrive safely in London, where they will stay at Matlock House."

"Matlock House!" At that moment, Georgiana and Ben entered the room, but her ladyship would not be deterred from having her say. "Nonsense, Darcy! Why should Georgiana and young Ben travel to London, and thus deprive me of their company, when they might remain here?"

Ben's expression quickly shifted from happy and carefree to bothered and concerned. He raced to Darcy's side and took him by the hand. "No, Da! I do not wish to remain here without you and Mama."

"Quiet child," said Lady Catherine. "Your wants are not what is being debated at the moment. In fact, the wants of a child can have no bearing on this discussion whatsoever. Georgiana, accompany young Ben outside to enjoy the fresh air while this matter is being decided."

Georgiana looked at her brother, seeking permission. Darcy nodded. Georgiana reached her hand out to Ben. "Ben, what say you we head out to the stables to have a look at the new colt?"

Ben did not budge. "Da, please do not leave me here. You know how I never wish to be parted from you and Mama. What if I should never see you again? What if—"

Darcy lowered himself to Ben's level and placed his hand on his son's shoulder. "Ben, you must never worry that either your mother or I will ever leave you. Now, run along with Georgiana. I shall come out and join the two of you once I have spoken with Lady Catherine."

Georgiana walked over to Ben and extended her hand once again. He accepted it, with some hesitation. Georgiana spoke softly to her brother, "I have no wish to remain here in Kent either, for what it is worth, however, I will not venture to speak for Anne except to say that this *is* her home." Darcy lifted a cautioning finger to his young sister, who merely shrugged. She looked at Ben. "Shall we be on our way, young sir?"

Ben smiled. "Yes, my lady."

When the two of them were gone away and beyond the hearing of the conversation at hand, Darcy said, "Lady Catherine, it was completely unnecessary for you to broach such a topic and cause my son to worry needlessly."

"What on earth are you saying, Darcy? Does the child being your son not make him my own great nephew? Why should he not be allowed to remain in my charge for a longer visit? Why, your own mother and father were perfectly content to have you remain here in Kent under my authority when you were the child's age. Is he somehow to be considered more precious than your own parents deemed you to be?"

"It is not that, your ladyship. Ben does not know you; hence, he suffers discomfort with the notion of staying here while his mother and I travel to Hertfordshire."

"It is about time we rectify that situation, is it not? Besides, soon enough the child will be separated from you and his mother, or does she plan to educate him herself, much the same as she was reared as a child—in a household of five daughters with no benefit of a governess."

Elizabeth entered the room in time to hear Lady Catherine's tirade. "If you suppose that such unsolicited attacks upon me will facilitate a favourable outcome in terms of allowing Ben to remain in your charge, you are sadly mistaken. What is more, how my son is educated is none of your concern, your ladyship."

Her ladyship's expression tightened. "Why, I never!" said Lady Catherine, her voice swelling with indignation. "It is no wonder young Ben suffers no compunction against speaking his mind with you as his mother. It is all the more reason that he should be allowed to stay with me, so he might learn to respect his elders. He needs to remember his place as a child."

Darcy's eyes turned cold and his voice icy. "I have heard quite enough, Lady Catherine. I know perfectly well how you feel. Should matters ever reach such an extreme, then I will remember your grand offer. In the meantime, let us get back to the matter of our immediate departure from Kent."

Lady Catherine's mouth gaped. "Immediate departure?"

"Surely you understand why my wife wishes to be by her father's side as soon as can be."

"As though your presence will make any difference," her ladyship said, ambling to her favourite chair.

Elizabeth looked daggers at the older woman. Darcy placed a calming hand on hers. "I have heard all I plan to hear on this matter, your ladyship." He looked in Elizabeth's eyes. "Pardon my aunt's rudeness, my love." Raising her hand to his lips, he bestowed a tender kiss on her knuckles. "Let us be on our way." Darcy turned to his cousin. "I leave it to you to make speedy arrangements for my family's removal to London."

Later, Darcy came across Georgiana and Ben in the stable yard. They raced to his side. "Brother, has all been decided?"

He squeezed his sister's hand. "Indeed. If you will, I would ask for a moment alone with Ben." She readily acknowledged her brother's need to speak with his son, and with a quick curtsey she walked away.

"Da, why is Lady Catherine trying to make me stay here at Rosings Park with her?"

"Ben, you must not worry about that. My aunt—actually *our* aunt—is very set in her ways. She is not used to anyone not going along with her plans. She means well. She always believes her intentions are good; however, I know from my own experience that such is not always the case. It is for that reason I shall never leave you or my sister in her charge."

"Then does that mean that we shall remain here at Rosings Park together?"

"Actually, preparations are being made for your mother's and my imminent departure as we speak. We have received news from Hertfordshire concerning your grandfather Bennet's health. Your mother is eager to arrive in Hertfordshire so she might be by his side. Cousin Richard will see Georgiana and you safely to town."

"But I should like very much to see my grandfather as well."

"I know you would, Ben. We all want to see him. However, in the interest of time, it will be best if your mother and I go on ahead. Once the situation is better understood and proper arrangements can be made for our entire party to remain in Hertfordshire—possibly for weeks—your cousin Richard will bring you and Georgiana to join us."

"What about Cousin Anne? Will she come with us?"

"I suppose that is entirely up to her. This is her home."

"Yes, Da, I know this is her *house*, the place she grew up. But does that make it her *home*?"

"Those are strong sentiments for one as young as you. Who have you been listening to?"

"It is what has been said for as long as I can recall. When Mama and I were at Longbourn, she often said it was a house that no longer felt like home. When we stayed in town with Uncle and Aunt Gardiner, Mama said it was a house that was not our home. She even said the same thing when we stayed with Aunt Georgiana in town. However, Cousin Anne often has said that Pemberley feels like home."

"Ben, tell me that you feel the same way—that Pemberley is home."

"I do, and you, Mama, Aunt Georgiana, Cousin Anne, and I are a family."

"Then I know what must be done, for we shall not have our family disrupted. What say you we go to Anne to make certain that she knows she is more than welcome to join us should she wish it? You do understand that she might wish to stay here at Rosings with Lady Catherine?"

"We shall never know for certain unless we ask her."

In spite of the gravity of their situation, Darcy chuckled. "I believe you are correct. Shall we proceed?"

Ben placed his hand in Darcy's and commenced urging him along. "Oh, yes. Let us do everything in our power to keep our family together."

Chapter 8

"Lizzy, Mr. Darcy, it is so good you have come. Perchance your presence will be just the thing to bring your father around. Oh, I pray that is the case. Your brother Geoffrey has been a true prince in taking over in your father's stead, but I should very much like to see Mr. Bennet recover." Clutching a linen handkerchief, Mrs. Bennet placed her hand on her chin. "I do believe I would be quite lost without him."

"Oh, Mama, I pray that what you say is true—that my being here will make a difference."

Geoffrey Collins and Jane came into the parlour to greet the Darcys, the former looking like the head of the village. Tall and exceedingly handsome, he and Darcy merely nodded at each other. Jane and Elizabeth rushed into each other's comforting embrace.

"Lizzy, it is so good you have come."

"Yes, Jane. It is good that you are here as well. How is Papa? Has there been any change in his condition? I should like very much to see him."

Before Jane replied, Elizabeth looked back at Darcy. "Are you coming with me?"

Darcy nodded. "If that is your wish."

"I do not know that I can do this without you." It was enough said. Darcy walked to Elizabeth's side, took her hand in his, and the two of them headed up the stairs to Mr. Bennet's room.

What Elizabeth saw, upon entering her father's room, took her breath away. Instead of the hearty robust man whom she had last welcomed to her home at Pemberley with such warm delight some months ago at Christmas, she espied what could best be described as a shell of her father. How pale and weak he looked. She silently vowed she would remain close by his side until he fully recovered. This was her father and, in spite of all their differences over the years, she felt strongly that she owed him as much.

Darcy took hold of his wife's elbow to steady her. They walked closer to the bed. Elizabeth leaned down and kissed her father's forehead. "Papa, I am here."

For a time, Darcy sat with his wife and offered whatever comfort he could as she busied herself attending her father. Once the sun had all but disappeared from the sky, Darcy said to Elizabeth. "Will you pardon me, my love, while I speak with my man to see that arrangements have been made for our stay in Meryton?"

Jane, who was happening by the partially opened door, entered the room. "Pray forgive me, but I could not help overhearing you. There is no need for you to stay in Meryton. I have seen to it that the two of you are settled in the green room." She said, "I apologise that the room is not up to your standards. The house is rather crowded, you see, and we all have to make allowances."

"You need not have gone to the trouble. Mrs. Darcy and I do not mean to disrupt the household."

"Nonsense, Mr. Darcy—it is unheard of that you should even think to stay in Meryton when there is no reason at all that we all should not stay here at Longbourn."

Elizabeth said nothing during the discussion. She was perfectly content to remain in the chair beside her father's bed if it meant being close to him. Her hasty departure from Kent had not been without immense distress over the prospect of leaving Ben behind. How her heart ached over the uncertainty of not knowing when they would be reunited. Still, she could not help but consider that their scheme to arrive in Hertfordshire ahead of Ben, Georgiana, and Anne was for the best. She missed him terribly. What a brave little lad he had been through it all, going so far as to pen a letter to his grandfather—all on his own. Elizabeth was close to tears when he handed it to her.

In truth, there was very little Elizabeth could do now, other than sit and pray and read. Her father loved nothing more than a good, long book. What pleasure he derived in immersing himself in one, especially a mystery.

Darcy placed his hands on his wife's shoulder. He applied a gentle massaging pressure. "We have been sitting here for some time. What say you to pausing for dinner?"

"I do not feel the least bit hungry, but you must not feel obliged to forgo dinner."

"I must insist you join me. There is no point in you sacrificing your own health. What purpose might that serve?"

Elizabeth reluctantly conceded to her husband's demands. Of course, he was correct. She would be of no use to anyone if she did not keep up her own strength. Her stomach's rumbling unceremoniously bolstered her decision. She needed a bite to eat after all. But just a quick bite, and then she would return to her father's side.

Standing, Elizabeth released her papa's hand and turned to her sister. "Jane, what exactly does the physician have to say about Papa's condition?"

"That is the hardest part about this, Lizzy, for Mr. Jones is at a complete loss to explain what brought about Papa's illness. Papa was found days ago lying here in much the same state as you see him now."

Darcy said, "May I ask who is Mr. Jones? Is he the man who attended you when you fell ill at Netherfield?"

"Indeed. Mr. Jones is the only person in Meryton who is to be consulted on such a matter as this."

"I shall consult my own physician. He should be in a position to make a more comprehensive assessment of this illness that has beset Mr. Bennet."

Geoffrey Collins entered the room in time to hear Darcy's proclamation. "Your generosity is most appreciated, but I am afraid it is entirely unnecessary. I have made arrangements to bring in a specialist from town. He shall arrive tomorrow."

"You are well within your rights to consult anyone whom you wish, just as I am within my rights to act accordingly."

Elizabeth and Jane exchanged knowing glances. Already their husbands were at odds, and the Darcys had only just arrived. Suspecting this was the first of many differences of opinions that lay ahead, Elizabeth fought not to roll her eyes to the ceiling. *And so it begins.*

* * *

Darcy looked around the tiny quarters. His man stood silently by the door. "If I did not know better, I would say that Collins had a hand in the selection of this room." In a tone meant only for himself, he said, "That pompous bore seems to have wasted no time at all designating himself head of the family in Mr. Bennet's stead."

The two small beds separated by a bed table would never do. Darcy turned to his man, Waters. "Mrs. Darcy and I will remain at Longbourn for as little time as feasible while Netherfield is being prepared. Please do what you can to see that this room is suitable to our needs—starting with the beds."

"Shall I have another bed—perhaps a larger one—brought up, sir?"

Darcy waved his hand. "It is entirely possible that these beds will suffice; however, the arrangement does not suit. How do you find your own accommodations?"

"There is not much room, what with the deluge of additional staff from both Lincolnshire as well as Pemberley, but I am certain we shall all manage during the brevity of our stay.

"Once you have seen to the rearrangement of this room, I would have you head over to Netherfield Park and oversee the preparations for our arrival. I am sure I do not need to tell you what all that entails."

"No, sir. I have a fine idea of your requirements."

"Good man," Darcy said and then headed out the door into the hallway to make his way back to Elizabeth's side.

* * *

The next day, Geoffrey Collins involved himself with the arduous task of poring over Longbourn's accounts. Always fastidious, he was rattled by the disorderly chaos of Mr. Bennet's library.

Tapping his fingers on the cluttered desk, he released a heavy sigh. *It is bad enough that it will require a small fortune to bring the management of the estate under control; I must also see to the refurbishing of the manor house.* In addition, there was the added expense of bringing a physician from town to oversee Mr. Bennet's care. As matters of wealth—or rather, lack thereof—robbed him of his tranquillity, so did thoughts of Longbourn's newest houseguest. Collins had been more aggrieved by Darcy's presumptuousness regarding consulting a specialist from town than he had let on.

By all accounts, that gentleman never deigned to set foot in Longbourn before yesterday. He thinks he will arrive and start directing matters according to his wishes.

It is only proper that I should make the decisions on behalf of the Bennets in Mr. Bennet's stead. My only question is why Darcy would even presume otherwise. "What of it that he has over ten thousand pounds a year and he owns half of Derbyshire?" Collins muttered. "Neither of those things are of consequence in this situation." He leaned back in the chair. *I am Mr. Bennet's heir. I am married to Mr. Bennet's eldest daughter. As long as Mr. Bennet is incapacitated, and certainly after he is no longer with us and as long as the Bennet daughters as well as Mrs. Bennet reside at Longbourn, I am their protector. I will not have an outsider dictate the management of my own home.*

Speaking to no one in particular, for he was the only one in the room, Collins said, "Should the proud Fitzwilliam Darcy of Pemberley in Derbyshire raise any objections, he may very well carry his point by removing Mrs. Bennet and her unmarried daughters into an establishment that he owns—even the great halls of Pemberley if it comes to that." Remembering the magnificence of the place and still smarting that anyone should live in the lap of such luxury, Collins huffed. "It is not as though he does not have the room."

* * *

Gillian and Emily raced into the parlour, just ahead of Elizabeth's next eldest sister, Mary.

"Where is young Ben? Does he remain in Kent with Lady Catherine de Bourgh?"

"Good morning, young ladies," said Elizabeth as she proceeded to give each of them a loving hug. "Ben is in London."

"Why did you not bring him with you? I should hate to think he is in London with complete strangers," said Gillian.

"Actually, Ben is with his aunt Georgiana and his cousin Anne. They are hardly strangers. And you remember the colonel, do you not?"

Bright smiles covered the girls' faces—likely a consequence of his having spent time entertaining them when they were all at Pemberley at Christmas. They nodded in perfect timing. Elizabeth said, "Colonel Fitzwilliam will see that the three of them are settled at Matlock House today."

Elizabeth's next eldest sister, Mary, adjusted her spectacles. "Why Matlock House? I am sure they would have been welcome to stay here at Longbourn, although the house is rather crowded what with Jane and our brother Geoffrey and Gillian and Emily and their governess." Mary went silent for a moment. "I suppose we could have—no, on the other hand…"

Elizabeth said, "Now, you understand my decision perfectly well for you have illustrated it yourself. Mr. Darcy and I rightly anticipated that there would be no room for our rather large party. Arrangements will be made to accommodate us all, and then Colonel Fitzwilliam will bring everyone to Hertfordshire. Ben sends his love, and he told me to tell you that he looks forward to seeing you again."

This was information enough to bring a warm smile to Mary's face. Elizabeth knew that Mary knew that, of all his Bennet aunts, she was Ben's favourite and for good reason too. She was the aunt who always treated him best, taking time to read to him, even if it was Fordyce's Sermons, as well as spending hours with him discussing his own favourite books from time to time. Certainly neither of the two younger sisters, Lydia and Kitty, could be bothered with their young nephew. Elizabeth had little doubt that Ben had as much use for them as they had for him. But his Aunt Mary—well, she was special to him.

Mary said, "How wonderful. I pray we shall see each other soon. Ben's liveliness might be just the thing that is needed here at Longbourn."

"I am apt to agree with you. In the meantime, he will be safe and protected with Lord and Lady Matlock in town."

Jane set aside her mending. "So, it is true that Mr. Bingley is returning to Netherfield and that you mean to reside there during your stay, as opposed to remaining with the family at Longbourn."

"Surely you can understand that our party is large and has strained Longbourn's resources considerably."

"Oh, Lizzy, you know that is all inconsequential where family is concerned."

Elizabeth huffed. "I am afraid my husband will disagree." *As will your own husband if I know anything about him at all.*

Chapter 9

Richard called on Matlock House for an early afternoon visit. The first person whom he encountered was his father, Lord Edward Fitzwilliam, the Earl of Matlock. He had missed seeing his father when he accompanied Ben, Georgiana, and Anne to the Grosvenor Square mansion earlier that week.

"Richard, how good it is to see you, son. I am sorry to hear about the Bennet family's travails. This cannot be an easy time for them."

"Indeed. Elizabeth was especially hard struck by the news. I want to say, on Darcy's behalf, how appreciative he is that you and mother are able to look after Georgiana and Ben while arrangements are being made to bring them to Hertfordshire."

"Think nothing of it. We are happy, even if a bit surprised, to be of service."

"Surprised, my lord? In what respect?"

"Surely you are no stranger to the contentiousness that has long marred the relationship between Darcy and me. I do believe this is the first time he has ever prevailed upon me to do anything for him."

"You must admit that things are vastly different now that you are no longer determined to dictate whom he should or should not marry. In addition, he is a father now, and I know he wants nothing more than to give young Ben a strong sense of family, even stronger than Darcy himself enjoyed as a child."

"Yes, that is very clear, as evidenced by that rather odd gathering at Pemberley at Christmas."

Richard strolled over to the drinks cabinet and began filling a glass. "What a festive occasion that was, but if you recall, we have Ben to thank for gathering us all together."

Lord Matlock joined him. "Yes—yes, indeed." Changing the subject, his lordship said, "Your cousin Anne is looking particularly lovely. I was very pleased to see that she did not remain at Rosings. Although, I can imagine my sister did not take too kindly to the development."

"Lady Catherine was not pleased but, then again, Anne is of an age where she must choose her own comings and goings."

"True—true, Anne is a fortunate young woman. It is a shame that she has not married. Then she might secure an arrangement of a more lasting convenience than that afforded by her stay at Pemberley."

Richard threw back his drink in a single gulp and poured another. "I suspect I know where this is going, my dear, matchmaking father."

"And why should I not make it clear that a match between you and Anne would be most advantageous for both of you? It spares both of you the time and trouble of a long and protracted courtship. Neither you nor Anne is getting any younger. Surely Anne will wish to have children."

"Having witnessed first-hand the love Darcy has for his wife and what a difference it has made in his happiness, I am thinking I want the same thing for myself. I do not know that I would enjoy such a life with my cousin."

"Surely you do not compare yourself to Darcy. He is a very rich man, thus he was able to marry where he would with no thought of the wife's fortune. Besides, if I know anything at all about my nephew, he is firmly in control of young Ben's inheritance by now." Lord Matlock took a sip of his drink. "You, on the other hand, must marry a woman of large fortune if you wish to maintain the manner of living to which you are accustomed, and Anne's fortune is magnificent."

* * *

Darcy stood in almost the exact spot where he and Ben had first met, engrossed in discussion with a local carpenter. Time was of the essence if his surprise for Ben would be ready when he arrived in Hertfordshire. He had planned to keep it a secret—even from Elizabeth. So much for the best laid plans. Hours earlier, Darcy had been working at a table in front of the window of their small apartment, when Elizabeth tiptoed behind him and tried to peep over his shoulders. Her soft breath against his neckline, as pleasing as it was, prompted him to roll up the parchment in haste.

"What are you studying with such intent, my love?"

"I did not expect to see you so soon. I supposed you to be with your father."

"I came to retrieve my book." She reached for the parchment. "What is this?"

Darcy tucked it behind his back. "This is meant to be a surprise."

"A surprise? For me?"

"Actually, it is a surprise for Ben."

"How wonderful. May I see it?"

"You will soon enough. I plan to unveil it to both of you soon after Ben's arrival."

Elizabeth eased her way into his lap, wrapped her arms around his neck, and nibbled his ear. "Please, my love, do not keep me in suspense."

"Is this your plan—to use your feminine wiles to bend me to your will?"

Elizabeth traced her tongue slowly along his earlobe. "How am I doing?"

What a dilemma his wife had posed. His special project was in jeopardy of being the furthest thing from his mind. "Can you keep a secret?"

"Of course, I can."

Darcy removed the parchment from behind his back and uncurled it. Elizabeth's mouth fell open upon taking it all in.

"I know what you are wondering. Let me assure you, it is safe."

"Oh, I would not think otherwise. No—I am astonished, that is all. Ben will love it."

"That is my thought exactly. Its construction is underway as we speak." Darcy placed the rendering on the table and stood with his wife in his arms, carried her to the closest of the two small beds, which were more conveniently rearranged for his purposes, and commenced bestowing upon her his undivided attention.

Her soft moans had given him to know he would be late in meeting the builder for their scheduled appointment. One satin covered button by one, Darcy slowly unfastened his wife's gown. He could not imagine committing such an unprofessional breach in etiquette for a less worthy cause.

※ ※ ※

Georgiana knew without being told the purpose of her aunt's early morning summons. Revered amongst her society acquaintances, Lady Ellen was heartbroken upon learning that her niece had eschewed coming out that spring. It was time for Georgiana to take her proper place amongst society's elite, and her ladyship told her niece as much.

Georgiana crossed her arms over her bosom. "I suppose this is your polite way of telling me it is time I find a husband—preferably a titled one should you and my uncle have your say and a wealthy one should my brother have his."

"Mind your tone, young lady. I am sure your brother and uncle want what is best for you—as I do."

"I beg your pardon, your ladyship. I have had this discussion so many times before with my brother and Elizabeth, even Lady Catherine."

"That is all the more reason to take this matter seriously. With that being said, I have written to your brother, expressing my concerns. He wrote back with his assurance that we are of the same mind on this subject. You will have your presentation at court and your coming out next year."

"So, I am to have no further say at all as regards my own future?"

"What reason might you have to possibly object to this scheme? Is this not what every young lady dreams of?"

Georgiana said nothing. She was not about to tell her aunt about her tacit understanding with the son of her late father's steward, Mr. Wickham. There was no need to subject the grand lady to a fit of apoplexy.

"Well, young lady, what have you to say further on the matter?"

There was really only one easy way to end their line of talk—feigning submission. "I know what is expected of me. I am exceedingly delighted about my coming out Season." Going further to add that she could hardly wait would have been stretching the truth a bit too far. Instead, Georgiana asked to be excused.

* * *

Each morning at Matlock House brought a new adventure into young Ben's daily routine. Still, he missed his parents dearly. The added uncertainty of his grandpapa's health weighed on him as well. He needed to do something to help his family, and he had just the thing in mind.

His lordship entered the study and, to his surprise, found the room occupied. "What on earth are you doing in here, young man?" Lord Matlock's booming voice was enough to frighten the poor child. Ben recoiled, knocking the inkwell over, and in so doing created quite a muddle of things.

"Look at my desk!" Lord Matlock marched across the room and pulled the bell for a servant.

"I am sorry, my lord!"

"As well you should be! I asked you what you are doing in here."

"I am writing a letter."

By now, his temple throbbing, his eyes bulging, his lordship stood directly before Ben. "A letter!"

"Yes, my lord, to my grandpapa in Hertfordshire."

His lordship observed the ink stains on Ben's hands and various parts of his clothing. He picked up the letter. "This looks like the work of a child."

Ben's face clouded with puzzlement. "I *am* but a child, my lord."

"Yes-yes, so you are. Why did you not get your aunt Georgiana or your cousin Anne to assist you in your letter writing campaign? I am sure the results would have been better than this." He looked at the splashes of ink all over the place. "It surely could not have been worse."

"Letters are meant to be private, are they not?"

"Some letters, letters of business and letters between adults, but as your letter does not fall into either of those categories, I do not see that any privacy is needed."

"Will you help me, my lord?"

"Me? I do not even know your grandfather!"

"Of course you do. You met him at Pemberley. Have you forgotten?"

"But of course—but how do you suppose I might help?"

"Surely my grandpapa and you have much in common. My friend Samuel and I are the same age, and we have much in common, and my grandpapa and you are the same age, so that means you two have a lot in common."

Lord Matlock huffed. "I am the Earl of Matlock. I am sure there is nothing common about me."

When the servant arrived, his lordship directed his attention to the ink spill, and the servant moved quickly to tidy things up.

"Is being the Earl of Matlock very important?" said Ben.

"I should say so!"

"Is it more important than being a grandpapa?"

His lordship jutted his aristocratic chin. "Being a grandpapa is not to be compared to being an earl. One has nothing to do with the other."

"What exactly does an earl do?"

"An earl has many important duties. I am a member of the House of Lords, the second house of Parliament. I give voice to the laws of the land and affect legislation."

Ben shrugged. "I suppose all those things are important."

"They most certainly are."

"But is it not also the duty of an earl to look after his family and see that they are protected and happy?"

"Yes—yes, there is that."

"Much like a grandpapa's duty is to look after his family and see that they are protected and happy."

"I shall not readily concede your point, young man. Anyone might be a grandpapa, but not every man is entitled to call himself an earl. One must be of noble blood to bear such a distinction."

Ben grew quiet as he considered his next words. By the looks of it, Lord Matlock was growing increasingly confident by the second that the child would not possibly have a retort that would justify any further discussions along those lines.

"My lord, if two men are walking together in the forest, and one of the men is of noble blood and the other is not, and they came across a ferocious fire-breathing dragon, which man do you suppose is more likely to fall prey to the dragon's attack first?"

His lordship curled his lip, and his steely eyes narrowed. Releasing a quick breath, he said, "Remove yourself from my chair and pull up a seat next to me, and tell me what exactly you wish to convey in this missive to your grandfather." After Ben took his place by his lordship's side, the elder man said, "By the bye, you do know there is no such thing as dragons, do you not?"

Ben tilted his head to the side. He could grow to like his great uncle very much, but he most certainly had his work cut out for him. *No such thing as dragons, indeed!*

Chapter 10

It was a certainty that the sympathy of every Meryton inhabitant was with the Bennet family, along with the hope for a speedy return to normalcy at Longbourn with the restoration of Mr. Bennet's good health. That the Bennet family's misfortune was the means of the return of a single gentleman in possession of a large fortune to the neighbourhood was also heralded as good news to all the eager mamas with unmarried daughters. Indeed, all of Meryton was talking about the goings on at Netherfield Park.

Charles Bingley's return to the country to be of service to his friend Fitzwilliam Darcy by opening up his home and accommodating the large Darcy party was further testament to his goodness. His ill-use of the former Miss Jane Bennet had long been forgotten pursuant to her marriage to the heir of Longbourn, and soon all the talk was that it was meant to be. All the local families were steadily planning who would be the first to invite the young man to dinner.

Soon after Bingley's arrival and the Darcys' subsequent removal from Longbourn to Netherfield, Darcy and Bingley sat in the finely-appointed parlour. Darcy advised Bingley once again that he need not have travelled to Hertfordshire for Darcy's convenience, saying that Bingley ought to be in London doing what young men did at that time of year, but Bingley had insisted that there was nowhere on Earth he would rather be.

"If I might speak frankly, Bingley," Darcy said.

Bingley settled back into his chair. "I do not recall a time when you did not speak your mind as you saw fit, my friend."

Crossing his legs, Darcy cleared his throat. "Yes, well—the fact is that your willingness to forgo the Season in town merely for the prospect of seeing Jane defies wisdom."

"Darcy, I know you feel it is a hopeless cause, but it is one for which I am bound. I shall never be satisfied with the way things ended between us. All I do is think of her, day and night. I adore her, and I long to be near her once again."

"But to what end, Bingley? As much as I do not care for the man, she is married to Collins, and from the looks of things, she is very content with her lot in life."

Bingley shrugged. "Yes, but being content is not quite the same as being happy."

"But being married is exactly the same as being married. I prefer to think you would never do anything to act on your tender regard for the lady."

"Trust me, Darcy; I would never do anything to dishonour your sister. However, no other woman has affected me quite like Jane. I doubt I will ever love another as I love her. I love her so much that it is enough for me to see her, to dine with her upon occasion. Surely I will have many opportunities to enjoy her company."

"And you are content in the knowledge that things between you will never be more—can never be more."

"I am."

* * *

Days after Ben's reunion with his parents, he, Darcy, and Elizabeth headed out on horseback towards the outskirts of the Longbourn estate. They had not journeyed far before brightly coloured flags of nearly every shade in the rainbow lining either side of the lane as far as Ben's eyes could see soon taught him to expect something magical. Recalling Darcy's promise to make amends for the shortened visit at Camelot, he could not wait to see what his father had in store for him. Travelling along the exact lane that would lead them to his and Darcy's favourite meeting place only added to the suspense.

Ben's eyes opened wide when he espied high in the sky a medieval fortress with ribbons in vivid hues of red, blue and green fluttering in the morning breeze saluting their approach.

Upon reaching their destination, Ben observed two knights in shining armour stationed either side the foot of the mighty tree. *Are they real?*

Ben jumped down from his pony, and a servant quickly stepped forward and guided it away. So excited was Ben, that he hardly knew where to look first. True to life knights hovered over him. Ben took a measured step back. *They are real!*

His heartbeat pounded. "My king, my queen—come and see what I see!"

Darcy dismounted his horse and quickly went to assist Elizabeth to the ground.

"Fitzwilliam, I had no idea that your plans entailed all this."

"I want Ben to be sufficiently entertained while we remain in Hertfordshire."

"Indeed, he will be. We must consider ourselves fortunate should we even see him after today."

Ben scampered up the wooden steps spiralling from the base of the tree to the fortress to have a look inside. There in the middle of the dwelling was a large, round table that looked as if it were fashioned from an ancient oak. Much to discover and delight the young lad lay all about: a coat of arms, two makeshift swords, a wooden treasure chest, the contents of which Ben could hardly wait to ascertain, a chain mail vest, its purpose solely for display, and even a throne fashioned from tree limbs and twigs. Ben could well imagine spending all his time there with his king. Shuttered windows on either side next drew his attention, and he raced over to the one closest, unfastened the latch which was meant to bar intruders from seizing the throne, and threw open the shutters. What a spectacular sight this particular window afforded, an unobstructed view of the land for as far as the eye could see.

From Ben's vantage point, his parents looked to be miles and miles away. Cupping his mouth, he said, "King Arthur, Queen Guinevere, you must come join me."

Once Darcy and Elizabeth were inside the fortress walls, Darcy moved about freely and comfortably. He imagined himself spending quite a bit of time with Ben and he was of an age where comfort trumped any other considerations. He opened the trunk and retrieved another surprise for Ben.

Handing it to Ben, he said, "I believe these will aid you in your quest, young sir."

Ben had never possessed anything quite like it but, having read about such a thing, he had a fair idea of its purpose. "My very own spyglass! Oh, thank you, sir." He raced to the opened window and held it up to his eye. His expression clouded. "I fear I see much better without it."

Darcy took the shiny black instrument from Ben and turned it around. Handing it back to Ben, he said, "Try this."

Ben did as Darcy directed and he was amazed. "Look—I can see all the way to Netherfield!" He immediately raced to the opposite side of his fortress and threw open the other window. After raising his spyglass to his eyes and taking in the new prospect, he said, "Queen Guinevere, there is Longbourn House! Come and have a look!"

Ben graciously displayed the proper use of his spyglass to his mother before handing it to her. "Sir Lancelot, it is indeed Longbourn." She returned the spyglass to Ben. "I should very much like to stay here and enjoy exploring your new kingdom, young sir, but I fear I must be away for my sisters are expecting me."

Ben looked through his shiny new instrument again and beheld another spectacle. "Look! Just over there. I see a crowd gathered." Countless brightly coloured streamers adorning covered tables and chairs lent a festive air to the prospect below. "It looks like a great feast!"

Darcy looked at Elizabeth sheepishly. "You must eat, my love."

Paying no mind to whatever his parents were discussing, Ben darted down the wooden steps and hurried off in the direction of the merriment.

Once there, he saw Colonel Fitzwilliam and Georgiana. "Merlin! What is all this?"

"What does it look like, Sir Lancelot?"

"It looks like fun! I am delighted you are here." He turned to his aunt and bowed. "My lady."

"Come now, Sir Lancelot. Surely you have surmised the perfect appellation for this angelic creature."

Georgiana smiled and clasped her hands in anticipation, while Ben contemplated the matter. "Forgive me, fair lady. Indeed, you are such a treasure. You shall be known as Anna, sister of King Arthur."

Arm in arm, Bingley and Anne approached them.

"Mr. Bingley! Cousin Anne!" Ben placed his fingers on his chin and tapped his lips a few times. "Rather—Sir Kay and Blasine. Yes—Sir Kay, brother of King Arthur, and Blasine, sister of King Arthur. I think that shall do nicely." He turned to the colonel. "What say you, Merlin?"

"I heartily approve, Sir Lancelot."

Bingley's countenance clouded. "Merlin? Sir Lancelot?"

Georgiana said, "Oh, yes, Mr. Bingley. Only proper Arthurian appellations are allowed on such an occasion as this."

"I see, and how might I refer to my good friend Darcy when I see him? Or do I even need to ask?"

Darcy must have heard all this as he and Elizabeth approached the group. "King Arthur, my friend. And who might you be?"

Bingley said, "It seems I am to be called Sir Kay."

Darcy held up Elizabeth's hand. "Sir Kay, may I present the love of my life, my sun, and my stars—my lady, Queen Guinevere."

A trumpet sounded, heralding a start of the festivities, beginning with a feast. Everyone proceeded to the table, which was heavy-laden with assorted breads, fresh fruits, cheeses, and wine, and, in its centre, a wild boar's head perfectly fitted for the occasion. Once everyone had partaken of three courses while being entertained by two colourfully attired court jesters, two knights took their places at opposite ends of the battlefield.

The court jester, who wore a bright leotard—red on one side and black and white checkered squares on the other, approached the table. He outstretched his hands before Darcy. One held a black and white cloth; the other a red and black cloth. "Choose your warrior, sire."

Darcy immediately deferred to Ben, who sat on his right. Excited, Ben leaned forward and took the proffered red and black cloth. The jester presented the other to Darcy, and another jester stepped forward and encouraged Elizabeth, Georgiana, Anne, Bingley, and the colonel to reach inside his bag and retrieve a flag.

One by one, each chose their colour and, as a result, their stake in the battle. Elizabeth, who sat on Darcy's left, picked a red and black flag. Sitting on Ben's right, Georgiana selected a red and black flag as well.

At three to one; the odds were stacked against King Arthur. Sir Lancelot knew not to be too confident, for the battle—as it were—had not yet begun. The young lad mentally calculated the odds that he would indeed come out ahead with so many flags left unchosen.

Next, it was Anne's turn. Black and white.

Then, Bingley chose. Another black and white flag emerged.

Young Sir Lancelot's confidence waned, but not his hope. Colonel Fitzwilliam's pick would decide the final outcome. How Ben wanted his friend Merlin on his team. Else it would be him and two fair ladies waging battle against his king, a knight, a maiden, and a magician. Ben's mouth fell open when the colonel pulled out a black and white flag and waved it in the air.

Any disappointment Ben suffered faded quickly as he reconsidered his chances of emerging victorious. Yes, King Arthur's team was larger, but Ben had Queen Guinevere on his side. Ben gazed at his knight who stood at the ready on the battlefield. What an imposing prospect he and his warhorse afforded. Donned in red and black, the knight was fierce, sitting high upon his beautifully turned out stallion coated in red and black garb protecting his head, chest, and flanks.

There stood his opponent on the opposite end. King Arthur's colourfully attired knight and war horse stood just as proud and fierce. Winning the imminent battle was going to be difficult, but Ben was quite determined that his side would prevail.

With the sun high in the midday sky, Darcy gave the commanding signal. "Let the battles begin."

The knights commenced a fierce jousting match that saw both sides cheering to see who could out do the other. Ben's knight was jostled from his stallion, but refusing to surrender, he took up his sword and shield. The fiercest of ground battles ensued.

The thrashing and clanging of heavy metal swords against shields made for quite an exhibition. So excited was Ben that his enthusiasm propelled him from his seat. He stood in his chair and rallied his warrior on in the man-to-man combat. At last, Ben's warrior emerged the victor.

The battle won, the warrior presented Sir Lancelot with the other warrior's shield.

"Oh, Da! May I keep this? I should like to display it in my fortress with my other treasures."

"It is yours to do with what you will, son."

Georgiana asked, "What is this about a fortress, Ben? You must take me there."

Elizabeth said, "This indeed has been a wonderful diversion, but as much as I should like to remain here and enjoy the festivities, I really must take my leave."

She had hardly finished her speech before the victorious knight presented her with one perfect red rose. She brought it to her nose and breathed in its fragrance.

The warrior handed Georgiana a rose as well, and then presented one to Anne.

Elizabeth placed her hand on Darcy's. "This has been a wonderful morning, my love; however, if I do not return now, I fear I will be missed at Longbourn."

Ben turned to Darcy. "Pray you are not required elsewhere as well."

"No, Ben. I am at your command." Standing, he said, "Pardon me, for I shall see my beautiful queen off, and then I shall return."

Ben smiled. He went to his mama and took her hand. Bowing, he bestowed a light kiss. "I shall see you at sunset, my queen. Pray you will be safe in your travels."

Darcy took Elizabeth's hand and led her to a spot nearby where three musicians sat playing under a heavily shaded tree. While waiting for her horse to be brought around, he trimmed her rose and tucked it behind her ear. This gave him the perfect excuse for trailing his hands lingeringly along her long slender neckline. With his thumb, he gently persuaded her chin upwards while he leaned in and kissed her softly upon her lips.

"I truly wish you did not have to leave."

"Pray you understand."

"Yes, of course I do. You want to be with your father."

"I do not know that I can ever truly thank you for bringing so much joy into Ben's life."

"Your love is all the thanks I shall ever require."

"Oh, I do love you—with all my heart." Her sweet proclamation was more delightful than the music that filled the air.

Darcy and Elizabeth continued in that attitude until the sound of the approaching groomsman drew them apart. Once he got his wife off safely along her way to Longbourn Village, he turned in the direction of the others and merely observed the goings-on in contentment. Throughout the meal, Darcy could not help but discern Bingley's enthusiasm. The court falconer standing a short distance away particularly drew his friend's attention. He was not surprised to see Bingley, Ben, and Georgiana now gathered around, admiring the hooded falcon perched upon the falconer's gloved arm.

Anne was seated on a blanket near the musicians, enjoying a merry tune, and Colonel Fitzwilliam stood across the way speaking with the two knights, whose fond remembrance of Ben during his London disappearance was a strong inducement for their willingness to give of their time for the young lad's amusement.

Then, as if weighing his choices on whether to join Anne or speak with Darcy, the colonel struck upon the path leading to where Darcy stood. When they were nearly face-to-face, Colonel Fitzwilliam said, "You truly out did yourself, old fellow. I do not know that I have ever seen Ben as happy as he is today."

"He was awfully disappointed we did not enjoy an outing in Kent similar to the one we enjoyed during his first visit."

"Yes, he often recounts what a jolly good time you all had during the medieval tournament at Camelot. I would say you more than made up for any disappointed hopes he may have suffered when Elizabeth and you left Kent."

There is also the matter of his disappointment in being separated from his friend. Darcy saw no need to embark on that particular discussion with his cousin. He commenced walking towards the falconer, and the colonel did likewise. Darcy said, "I am glad you approve."

"Indeed. When did you manage to put this whole thing together? I had supposed you were engaging my men for a small exhibition. I never expected anything as grand as this. It looks as though you have half of Meryton at your disposal."

"I have given little thought to anything other than planning this day since Elizabeth and I arrived in Hertfordshire."

"Yes, I can imagine you have a prodigious amount of time on your hands what with Elizabeth spending so much of her time at Longbourn."

"I must confess that Longbourn is not my favourite place, which means I do not see my wife as often as I would like. I do not imagine I shall enjoy the pleasure of your company much longer either. When do you plan to return to town?"

"Not until I have accomplished the second half of my mission."

Raising his brow, Darcy said, "The second half of your mission? Other than deliver my family safely from town, I did not know you had a mission."

"Indeed."

"Would your mission have anything to do with Anne?"

"Anne?" Richard raised his hand in dismissal. "For heaven sakes—no!" Colonel Fitzwilliam commenced brushing invisible lint from his sleeve. "You know very well that I intend to renew my acquaintance with the lovely Mrs. Collins."

"Jane!"

"Indeed. You need not look so astounded. Did I not give you every indication of my sentiments when we were in Kent?"

"Jane? Do you not recall my saying she was content with her lot?"

"Oh, I remember perfectly well. However, nothing in your tone suggested she was happy."

"I surely did not mean to imply she was unhappy."

"I suppose I shall know soon enough."

Chapter 11

Two days later, when Darcy's business with his solicitors required a trip to town, he took Ben with him. By now, Elizabeth spent most of her time at Longbourn, so she might help out with the care of her father. There was always something or other that needed tending, and as Geoffrey Collins was not inclined to avail himself of all Darcy's extensive resources, everyone took turns doing what they could. Elizabeth mostly sat with her father, reading to him and talking to him about those remembrances of their past she knew would bring him pleasure. When she was not thus occupied, she was spending time with her mother.

Mrs. Bennet had been eerily quiet of late. One might even describe her as pensive. She was even content to allow her eldest daughter, Jane, to assume those duties inherent in being the mistress of Longbourn, despite Jane's repeated assurance that soon her father would be up on his feet again and the Collinses would return to their own home in Lincolnshire. Elizabeth thought if anything would lift her mama's spirits, it would be Bingley's return. What did her mother live for but to make favourable matches for her single daughters? Alas, the announcement of the gentleman's return was met with little more than a vague, unreadable smile.

Elizabeth's youngest sisters were not so apt to spend long hours by their ailing papa's bedside. Their youth, their energy, their poorly formed minds, as well as their heightened sense of their own significance made it impossible that the young girls would sit idly by in the manor house when there was the excitement of a walk to Meryton to entice them out of the house. On one such occasion, the girls had the honour of making the acquaintance of Mr. George Wickham.

Indeed, they introduced him to their aunt, Mrs. Philips, who in turn invited the dashing lieutenant and some of the other officers to dinner. So pleased were they over this triumph that Lydia and Kitty could hardly contain themselves when they pranced into the manor house and nearly collided with Elizabeth and Georgiana who were preparing to take their leave for Netherfield.

"Oh, Lizzy, Georgiana, you will never guess where we have been or with whom we were speaking."

"Do calm yourself, Lydia. Who has got you in such a state?"

"We have just met one of the officers. Oh, I declare he is the handsomest man in the world."

The girls joined hands and danced around. Kitty said, "Indeed. He is more handsome than Mr. Collins and Mr. Darcy!"

"Oh, Lizzy, you must come with us to dinner this evening and see for yourself, for Aunt Philips has invited all of us."

Now settled in the carriage, Georgiana said, "What say you, Elizabeth? Shall we dine at Mrs. Philips's this evening?"

"Georgiana, I do not know that it would be agreeable with your brother, given that you are not out in Society."

"Elizabeth, you know perfectly well that my brother never objected to my attending small family parties."

"Of course, those were parties at Matlock House. I suspect your brother would hardly equate dinner with my Meryton relatives to dinner with aristocracy. Then there is the fact that the officers from the militia will be there."

"It is not as though I have never dined with an officer before."

"Yes, but dining with your cousin Colonel Fitzwilliam does not count."

"Oh, Lizzy, please," Georgiana said in a voice meant to sound like Lydia's. Neither of them could help laughing. Once she resumed a more elegant air, Georgiana said, "Besides, my brother is in town with Ben. Is it not true that they will remain there until tomorrow? He need never know how we spent this evening."

Georgiana was nearly nineteen. Elizabeth would be lying if she said she agreed with her husband's rigid views of young ladies who were not officially out. Besides, she had been attending such dinner parties since she was fourteen. With all that in mind, Elizabeth was more than agreeable to the scheme. *Dinner at Aunt Philips's it shall be.*

Hours later, Georgiana was delighted to be the woman upon whom the dashing Lt. Wickham bestowed his smiles that evening. If only she could boast of having his undivided attention. Alas, she could not, for he seemed to take a very keen interest in Elizabeth as well. Georgiana would not complain. Being in his company with Elizabeth by her side provided the concealment she needed to avoid giving rise to speculation of an attachment between Georgiana and the gentleman. If such were to reach her brother Darcy's hearing, it would mean the end of her prospects before they even saw the light of day.

A great part of Georgiana wished desperately for time with George Wickham that evening. The many years since she had last seen him had been nothing but kind to him. His appearance was greatly in his favour; he had all the best part of beauty, a fine countenance, a good figure, and his address was as pleasing as she remembered it to be. *Oh, how handsome he is.*

For so long, she had been dreaming of him, waiting for him, just as he had asked her to do; however, he gave no indication of even remembering having uttered those words. *In fact, in Elizabeth's presence he is content to treat me as the same young girl that he used to spend hours entertaining so many years ago at Pemberley.*

It would not do. She was a woman. Her body's reaction to merely being in his company, even in a room full of people, was confirmation of that. *I must find a way to see him alone, outside of my sister's company, and then I will know how he feels about me and determine how I, in turn, feel about him.*

Darcy was livid!

He and Ben had returned from town earlier than planned and, wanting to surprise his wife, Darcy decided he would join her at the Philipses' dinner party. What he had espied upon his arrival filled him with disgust. He was aware of the militia's recent encampment just outside of Meryton, but he had no idea of its being George Wickham's regiment. The last time he had seen his former friend was at Pemberley. Soon after his father passed, Darcy had given Wickham the value of the living that the elder Mr. Darcy had wished for his godson when Wickham made it clear he had no desire to take orders. It was money well spent as far as Darcy was concerned, for Wickham was not a principled man. His being granted the living would have been a travesty. However, Wickham later returned when the living became available, insisting that it ought to be his. Darcy would not hear of it. Wickham countered, demanding even more money. Darcy refused. All subsequent discourse had been so tarnished with vitriol and vile accusations that Darcy exiled Wickham from Pemberley forever.

How dare that reprobate ingratiate himself with my wife and my sister? It was all Darcy could do not to upbraid his former friend in view of everyone, but as it was a family dinner party and they were merely conversing, Darcy held his tongue. Instead, he kept his distance. *Better I observe Wickham in order to know what he is about.*

Darcy suffered a restless night. Seeing Wickham with his family had bothered him more than he would have anticipated, especially seeing him with Georgiana. What if she held Wickham in as high esteem as had their father? She had no knowledge of Wickham's vile propensities. Perhaps she did not fully comprehend the depths of his distrust of George Wickham.

I have never told her what transpired between us. She only knows he is never to be received at Pemberley, for that is all I ever told her. Darcy intended to amend his lapse where his sister was concerned. *The sooner I counsel her on how to regard that scoundrel, the better.*

After breakfast the next morning, Darcy invited his sister to join him for a turn about the gardens. His purpose was two-fold: one, to spend time with her, for there had been very little of that of late, and two, to counsel her on how she ought to comport herself during their Hertfordshire visit. "I saw you talking with Mr. George Wickham at the Philipses' home last evening."

"I am sure you did. I spoke with many people at the dinner party. George was but one of them."

"George?"

"How might you expect me to address him? Did I not enjoy many pleasurable hours in his company when he resided with us at Pemberley?"

"That may be true, but referring to a gentleman by his given name implies a certain familiarity."

"Indeed, it does. But then again, George is much like family, is he not?"

Darcy's muscles tightened. Family was the last thing he considered that reprobate. If his sister only knew the scoundrel like he knew him, she too would be appalled. "Georgiana, I do not wish to have you spend time with George Wickham."

"Why ever not?"

"He and I did not part on the happiest of terms."

"What can that have to do with me?"

"I do not think I should have to explain myself, young lady. I would simply ask that you trust me."

"Did you fail to notice that he and your own wife were also engaged in rather amiable intercourse during parts of the evening? Have you given her the same admonishment?"

Darcy's face filled with astonishment. When had his young sister learned to speak to him in so unguarded a manner? "As Elizabeth is my wife, I do not endeavour to tell her with whom she can and cannot associate. It is quite a different matter when it comes to you, young lady. As your guardian, it is well within my rights to tell you with whom you are to associate, and I do not intend to abdicate those rights anytime soon."

Not wishing to do anything to perturb her beloved older brother, Georgiana thought it best to hold her tongue. She fully expected that her brother in all likelihood had spoken to Elizabeth about George, especially if he felt so passionately about the subject as to attempt to admonish her. She suspected Elizabeth had balked at his decree. Georgiana dared not be as bold with her brother as Elizabeth likely had been, but that did not mean she would heed her brother's edict as easily as he expected.

George means far too much to me. He asked me to wait for him, and that is exactly what I have done. Now, when I am finally of an age where he and I can be together, I intend to do everything in my power to see that we are—the wait is over.

As far as she was concerned, if an extended passage of time preceded her brother's knowledge of that fact, it was so much the better.

Darcy and Elizabeth sat across from each other in the library, embroiled in heated debate. They may as well have been on opposite sides of the world. How stubborn she could be when she chose.

"Please trust me on this, Elizabeth."

"Georgiana has known him all her life and she does not disdain him—quite the contrary."

"That is because she does not know his character as I do. She does not understand what he is capable of."

"But everyone whom he has met since being here has nothing but the highest regard for him."

"Wickham is blessed with such happy manners as to make friends wherever he goes. It is no wonder everyone is falling all over themselves to make love to him. However, he is unable to retain his easily earned esteem, and that is why I have no wish to have him connected to my family."

"I know that he has been so unlucky as to lose your good opinion, and I also know your good opinion once lost is lost forever, but is there no possibility in your mind to allow that he is not the same gentleman you once knew? People can change."

"People might change if that is their fervent wish, and they make a good effort. Wickham, however, is not the sort of person who would even wish to change. His greatest faults are those very attributes he regards as virtues."

"Please, sir, let us not discuss this matter of Mr. Wickham any longer. I shall keep an eye on Georgiana if that is what you wish, but I surely will not spy on her, and I will not violate her confidence either. I know you are Georgiana's guardian and you liken her to a daughter, but I posit that she is of an age where you would appreciate her far better if you start to consider her as a sister—as an adult sister, for that is certainly the basis of my relationship to her, that of sisters."

"You being a wiser, far worldlier sister," Darcy said.

"Is that your way of calling me old, Mr. Darcy?"

"Well, you are older than Georgiana, are you not?"

"By a few years—not decades, for heaven's sake!"

"Yes—I know. You are closer in age to her than not, and it is natural that you and she share a sisterly bond, whereas the bond between Georgiana and me is rather blurred." Darcy crossed the room, took Elizabeth in his arms, and rested his chin atop her head. He ran his hands along the length of her arms. Capturing her hand in his, he drew back a little; he looked into his wife's eyes. "Do you suppose that my sister regards me as being too severe where she is concerned? The last thing I want is to alienate her."

"On the contrary. She loves you very much, and it is evident that she thinks you are the best man in the world."

"I must confess that she is very wise in that regard."

"Of course," said Elizabeth teasingly.

"I would never ask you to spy on her or share your confidences with me, for it means everything to me that the two of you are so close. It is what I always wanted for her—to have a sister.

"I would ask you to help her, as best you can, to make good decisions for herself, especially when it comes to discerning the motives of the many men whose acquaintances she will be making."

Darcy wanted desperately to say that, just because certain behaviour was deemed acceptable for Elizabeth's younger sisters, it did not follow that it would likewise be acceptable for his own sister. He did not dare, at least not now. Still, he strongly suspected a conversation on the younger Bennet daughters' behaviour was one he ought to have, only not with Elizabeth.

Chapter 12

Darcy's stance towards Elizabeth's sisters in relation to his attitude towards Georgiana bothered him, keeping him up most of the night. It was only natural that he would feel more protective of the latter. He was, after all, more than her older brother; he was her guardian. He thought of himself as a father as much as a brother, whereas Elizabeth's sisters, well—he hardly knew them at all.

Given his first opportunity to make their acquaintance all those months ago at the Meryton assembly, Darcy had gone out of his way to avoid it. He was revolted by the spectacle the younger girls had made, standing before his friend Bingley and jousting for position to see which would be favoured with Bingley's attention. Darcy had once thought them the silliest creatures in the world—uncouth and uncivilised. Was his marriage to his beloved Elizabeth meant to change all that?

Knowing he had to do better, he decided that he would make an effort to be more of a brother to the younger Bennet sisters, Mary, Kitty and that wild Lydia. He owed it to his wife to try, at least, did he not? He vowed to head over to Longbourn first thing that morning and speak with Geoffrey Collins about the younger girls' propensity to admire George Wickham. He would strongly advocate that Collins, in his self-appointed capacity as head of the Bennet family in his father-in-law's stead, take control of the situation. He certainly did not look forward to that, for although he and the gentleman were civil, their mutual cordiality could be described as tenuous at best.

Upon his arrival at Longbourn, Darcy paced outside the library. Collins had the audacity to keep him waiting for a private audience. *How dare he?* Once they were seated face-to-face on opposite sides of Mr Bennet's desk, Darcy wasted no time in addressing his purpose in being there.

"Collins, I have a matter of a rather delicate nature that I wish to discuss with you. It has to do with the youngest Bennet daughters," he cleared his throat, "our sisters."

"I think I know what you are about to say, Darcy. It has not escaped my notice that the younger girls suffer the mischief of neglect and mistaken indulgence, but I believe I have already taken measures to rein them in. I have two young daughters of my own, and I am not at all pleased by the example the younger Bennet girls set."

"It seems that finally we have something we can agree upon."

"I would not go as far as that, but I will hear what you have to say."

"My immediate concern has to do with their wont of cavorting with the militia, specifically the officer named George Wickham."

"George Wickham? I do not believe you could be more mistaken." Collins leaned back in his chair. "If you mean to persuade me against him, you will meet with no success. The lieutenant is a decent, upstanding fellow who has been dealt an unfortunate injustice." Reaching for his pipe, Geoffrey Collins cleared his throat. "The gentleman and I embarked upon a lengthy discourse on his travails. I am certain I do not need to say more, for as intimate as you are with the gentleman, you can have no doubt of the nature of his grievances."

"I admit it does not come as a surprise to me that George Wickham would tell his version of our history to anyone who is gullible enough to believe what he has to say."

"It is not very hard to believe him when I have been the direct recipient of your displeasure myself."

"Pray, you are not clinging still to the notion that I am the reason you failed to secure Elizabeth's hand in marriage."

"Actually, all that is neither here nor there. All I am saying is that what Mr Wickham related is entirely in keeping with the man whom I know you to be. Hence, I will not listen to a word you have to say against the gentleman."

"I am sorry to hear you say that, for you have appointed yourself as head of the Bennet family, and along with that distinction comes the responsibility of protecting the younger girls, does it not?"

"I will not argue your point, and, as I have said, I have given this matter some thought. I assure you I have the situation under control."

"How so—if you do not mind my asking?"

"To be honest with you, Darcy, I do mind your asking. This is Longbourn, not Pemberley, and I will not be second guessed."

"It is a shame to hear you speak this way. We need not be adversaries, especially when it comes to a matter such as this. The girls' comportment is just as much of consequence to me as it is to you."

"And there is the point. What concerns you most is that Longbourn House might bring shame upon the *hallowed* Darcy name. How it must vex you not to be in control of every detail of your otherwise perfectly arranged life."

Of course it bothered him. Scandal of any kind was Darcy's abhorrence. The prospect of some disgrace that might befall either of the youngest Bennet daughters, bringing shame upon his family and affecting Georgiana's chances of marital felicity, was too much to hazard.

Darcy stood and prepared to take his leave. "I had hoped to find you reasonable. However, I see now that your own pride makes that impossible. You ought to know that I will be keeping watch over this matter. I will take whatever action I deem necessary to protect my family, regardless of anything you have to say."

Darcy might have known he would have no success at all in dealing with Geoffrey Collins, but it could not be said that he did not try. Although his mood was much darker when Darcy descended the front stairs and made his way across the paddock, the burden on his conscience was lighter by far.

Chapter 13

Days later, George Wickham approached Georgiana in the garden at Longbourn. He presented her with her favourite flower and proceeded to beguile her with reminiscences of their most cherished moments at Pemberley.

Georgiana was exceedingly entertained, and she made no pretence of hiding it. "You always did know how to make me laugh, George. Although, I suppose I should learn to address you otherwise for appearances sake and to lessen the aspect of familiarity that exists between us."

"But are we not especially familiar? Have I not known you all your life and I dare ask who knows me better than you?"

She smiled fondly at the person who had devoted so many hours to giving her pleasure over the course of her life. "If only my brother could summon the strong familial harmony you and he once shared."

"I take some of the credit for Darcy's hard feelings against me for, just before he and I parted company at Pemberley, I might have expressed my disappointment with him less violently than I did. I might have handled my temper much better, and I know that now. If I could do it again, I most certainly would do it differently, for I am a changed man, and soon Darcy will see that too."

He extended his arm, which she graciously accepted, and he guided her away from view of the manor house. "Seeing you alone in the garden was fortuitous. I have longed for a chance to speak with you in privacy. There is much I had wished to say to you when we dined with the Philipses that evening."

"And I you."

"I have thought of you so many times since we parted, and never more than of late, now that you are a young woman of an age where you are likely giving thought to your place in society. You do remember your promise that you would wait for me?"

Her heart turned somersaults. Her hopes and dreams had not been in vain, for he remembered their promise as well.

"And despite the disheartening circumstances that brought you to Hertfordshire, it is most fortunate that we are all here. Soon, your brother will come to know how mistaken he is about my character, and he will bless our future union."

"Oh, George, does that mean what I think? Are you? Are you?"

"I am indeed—if you will have me."

"Oh, nothing would satisfy me more."

"Then, it is official. Mind you, this must be our secret. We will know when the time is right to share our happy news with others."

* * *

As was her custom, Elizabeth had spent hours in her father's room, reading to him and the like. She was encouraged by what she felt certain were daily signs of improvement in his health. Having reached a fitting stopping point for the day, Elizabeth placed her book aside, stood, and walked to the window. She was not at all surprised to espy the dashing Lieutenant Wickham, for he and some of the officers regularly called at Longbourn. She was, however, surprised to see the gentleman and Georgiana sitting together on a bench. The couple's comportment hinted of a fair degree of intimacy. "How long has this been going on?" Elizabeth voiced aloud.

She cast a furtive glance over her shoulder. His breathing steady, Mr. Bennet's eyes were closed. Elizabeth proceeded to the door and quickly made her way outside. She was half way to the place where she had espied Georgiana and the lieutenant when she saw her sister headed towards the manor house—alone.

Elizabeth waited until they were but a short distance apart. "Georgiana, I saw you and Mr. Wickham in the garden earlier."

"Indeed, Elizabeth. He called on the Bennets while you were visiting with your father, and he joined me as I was having a turn in the garden so we might talk."

"Pardon, is this the first such instance where you and he have enjoyed a turn in the garden?"

"Come now, Elizabeth, I can well imagine my brother asking such a question. I am surprised to hear you voice it."

"I would be remiss if I did not ask. Your brother has made it clear that he does not approve of Mr. Wickham, regardless of how amiable you or I might consider him to be. He would be terribly disappointed if he knew that you were spending time in the gentleman's company."

"Then, do not tell him is all I can say. I believe my brother is being entirely unreasonable where George is concerned. I have known George all my life, and all my memories of him are happy ones. Having met him and even spent time in his company yourself, can you wonder why I simply adore him?"

Elizabeth drew her head back. "Adore him, you say?"

"Indeed, what is there not to adore about him? He is kind and considerate; he is what every gentleman aspires to be."

"He may be all those things, but pray you are not mistaking fondness built upon the basis of sweet childhood memories as something more."

Georgiana coloured. She stared. She said nothing.

Elizabeth said, "Pray you take my meaning."

Georgiana crossed her arms over her chest. "Perhaps you ought to just say what is on your mind."

"Georgiana, I pray you are not considering that your future is with Lieutenant Wickham."

"I see no reason why I should not be as happy with him as with any other gentleman."

"I am sure your brother would beg to differ."

"That is because my brother does not like George."

"I am afraid his displeasure in seeing you married to such a man would be based upon more than mere dislike."

Georgiana huffed. "I suppose you are alluding to the gentleman's lack of fortune, his want of connections. I know that, were I to entertain the notion of becoming Mrs. George Wickham, it would entail certain sacrifices. There would be no fine homes the likes of Pemberley and Darcy House, no fine carriages and such, but my own fortune is not insignificant, and as I think about it, as the sister of Fitzwilliam Darcy and the niece of the Earl of Matlock, on the whole, I shall have no cause to repine."

As Georgiana took in the raised brows of her sister, she began to consider that she had said too much, and she thought of tempering her strong sentiments just a little, for, after all, her tacit engagement with George had scarcely even begun. For now, it was meant to be a secret between the two lovers until the time was right to let others know, and she did not intend to force the issue by allowing her brother to gain wind of the situation before there indeed was a situation.

She was not unaware that, if her brother had his way, she would find herself married to his friend, Charles Bingley. She certainly liked Mr. Bingley well enough, but she would never say she adored him. Besides, Bingley had never looked at her even once, as best she could tell. He only had eyes for another—Elizabeth's older sister, Mrs. Geoffrey Collins.

"Mind you, Elizabeth, I am only putting forth such an argument to illustrate my point that the size of a man's fortune shall not be the deciding factor in my decision to marry. With that said, there is no reason at all for you to be concerned about my feelings as regards George, and, for heaven's sake, I would ask that you make no mention of any of this to my brother. I have told him already that I shall not allow his opinion of George to shape my own and further that he does not get to decide with whom I spend time. I think it is unreasonable for him to expect me to slight George simply because they suffered a misunderstanding.

"Besides, I know that he and George were once very close—I dare say the best of friends—when they were younger. Who is to say they will not one day put their differences behind them?"

Elizabeth placed her hand on Georgiana's arm. "One can only hope, but you know your brother, and he affirms that his good opinion once lost is lost forever."

"Indeed, I know his sentiments all too well, but I am a strong believer that everyone deserves a second chance. Pray my brother will come to feel that way too. I know it is something my dear father would have wished for—that Fitzwilliam and George should be lifelong friends. This rift between them would simply break his heart, for my father loved George as though he were his own son."

Chapter 14

As they sometimes did when there was no amusement to be enjoyed at Netherfield, Darcy and Ben ventured to Meryton that afternoon. When they stepped out of Ben's favourite shop and onto the street, the little fellow's attention was soon caught by the sight of some of his dearest acquaintances.

"Look, Da, my aunts are here in Meryton!"

"Where are they, Ben?"

"There!" he said, pointing the way. "Let us go over and greet them." Before awaiting a reply, Ben raced ahead of Darcy.

When Ben reached his aunts, he observed that they were not alone, but rather there were two gentlemen in their party. Ben stared into the face of the taller of the two men. "I believe I have seen you before, sir. Have you ever been to Pemberley?"

The tall, handsome stranger's face took on an air of amusement. "Indeed, I have. I spent the better part of my life at Pemberley." He extended his hand and said, "Lieutenant George Wickham at your service." Ben accepted the gentleman's proffered hand. Wickham said, "And who might you be?"

Darcy approached the party without greeting anyone. "Come along, Ben." Taking Ben by the hand, he led him away.

Ben's countenance clouded with confusion. Once they were a fair distance away, he tugged on Darcy's sleeve. "Da, did you not even recognise to whom I was speaking? It was the gentleman whose likeness is in your study. He called himself a lieutenant."

"Ben, I am well aware of the identity of the man to whom you were speaking. You have a very good memory to recall having seen his likeness amongst the miniatures at home. However, you must also recall my telling you that the gentleman is no friend of mine. I would have you keep your distance from him."

"He seems like a very nice gentleman. Why do you dislike him?"

"Ben, I trust you know better than to judge a book by its cover. I can think of no more fitting an illustration of that old adage than in the case of that gentleman. He is not at all as he seems."

"My aunts were all delighted by him as well. You did not admonish either of them to keep their distance."

Darcy's stomach muscles tightened. He had indeed spoken to his own sister to stay away from George Wickham, for all the good it had done. Even his own wife had been persuaded to think favourably of that reprobate. Of course, he had also spoken to Geoffrey Collins, urging him to caution the younger girls. His efforts had been in vain.

His voice calm, Darcy said, "Ben, the fact is that I would have you keep your distance from strangers in general. You are very young and, by and large, very trusting, but you are also very vulnerable, and there are many disreputable people whose intentions are not always good."

"But he is an officer. Are not all officers honourable and meant to protect everyone from harm? Colonel Fitzwilliam is very good. I have heard you say he is one of the best men you know."

"Yes, well, the gentleman who just introduced himself to you is no Colonel Fitzwilliam."

Darcy's displeasure over being in proximity with Wickham and his family's growing admiration of that scoundrel would not be repressed. He joined Elizabeth in her apartment later that evening. Finally, they were at liberty to discuss the events of the day with no fear of being interrupted. "I saw you in Meryton with Georgiana, today."

"Oh, why did you not come and speak with us? I should have enjoyed your company. There is a little shop that I am eager for you to visit with me."

"I saw the two of you speaking with George Wickham." He crossed his arms. "Need I say more?"

Elizabeth arched her brow. "I suppose you had better if you wish for me to understand your purpose."

"Ben and I were together. I had just escorted him away from that gentleman's audience earlier and admonished him against any further association with Wickham. I thought I had made my sentiments known to you as well."

"Mr. Darcy, Ben is a child, and if you mean to protect him from the likes of the *villainous* Mr. Wickham, that is your right; however, you cannot possibly expect me to heed your admonishments as easily as that, especially when my sisters were all standing there engaged in perfectly amiable discourse with the gentleman and his friend."

"However, you were with *my* sister, and I expect you to do my bidding when it comes to protecting her."

"Sir, you expect me to treat Georgiana as though she were a child. I will not be a party to it. Georgiana is not a child!"

"Why must you fight me on this? Your stance defies reason. Have you ever known me to be wrong about anything?"

"What a ridiculous thing to say in attempting to persuade me against my own purposes. Shall I defend myself by cataloguing your shortcomings?"

"*My* shortcomings?"

"Do you deny you like arranging things to suit your own convenience?"

"You sound like Geoffrey Collins!"

"In such a case as this, I know not whether to consider your assertion an insult or a compliment."

When had this become a discussion of my faults? Darcy took her by the hand, led her to the sofa, and silently urged her to sit next to him. "Must we talk about this now?"

"What shall we talk about?"

"Must we talk at all? I rarely see you anymore, what with all the time you spend at Longbourn—not that I am complaining about your spending time with your father, for that is the purpose in our being here in Hertfordshire, it is just that I miss you terribly."

"You might reconsider your stance and come with me to Longbourn upon occasion."

"You know that I would much rather not."

"Because of my brother, Geoffrey?"

"He and I have no use for each other. I imagine if I were to spend too much time at Longbourn, the two of us might come to blows. You would not want that."

"I suppose you have a point."

"Shall we make a pact, my love?"

"What are you proposing?"

"I propose that we do not spend another second talking about anyone who is not currently in this room, and focus solely upon each other—at least for the rest of the evening and well into the wee hours of the morning."

She opened her mouth to fashion a protest, but he placed a silencing finger to her lips.

"Just the two of us," he said, the titillating sensations of his lingering touch aiding him in his purposes. "I need you too."

"Well," said Elizabeth, leaning into his kiss. After a moment of relishing the ardent pleasures he bestowed, she sighed. "When you state your wishes so eloquently, how can I possibly refuse?"

Chapter 15

Prone to the unenviable iniquities of vanity and jealousy, Lydia sulked. Any occasion during which she found herself in the company of an officer donning a red coat who did not deem her the object of his ardent admiration was a source of a great deal of displeasure. Being slighted by one particular officer, especially in her own home, was unthinkable. Such an unsettling situation needed to be addressed, and Lydia possessed just the right combination of brashness and daring to see to it. Seizing her chance, she commanded his attention in a corner of the room.

"Mr. Wickham, I am extremely disappointed, for it appears to me that Georgiana Darcy thinks she has some manner of claim on you."

"Miss Lydia, it is a pleasure to see you too. How very considerate it is of you to seek me out this evening at a time when I supposed I would be competing with all the other officers for the pleasure of your company."

"Sir, all the flattery in the world will be wasted should you persist in bestowing it merely to change the subject."

"Yes, well, you will recall my saying that Miss Darcy and I grew up at Pemberley. Although I am older than she is, she remembers our time together with such great affection. I like to do whatever I can to pay her those little compliments that young ladies enjoy hearing."

"So, you do not like her?"

"On the contrary, I like her very much."

"But, I suppose what I mean to say is, do you love her?"

"Why are you asking me all these questions, Lydia? How can I possibly love her when you have stolen my heart and ruined me for all other women?"

"If that is true, then when do you suppose we shall be married?"

He coughed. "Married? So, you think you should like to get married? Do you not suppose that you are rather young to even consider such a scheme?"

"Oh, no! On the contrary, it is all I ever think about. In fact, I spend my days and nights dreaming about it."

He bit his lower lip. "Days *and* nights, you say? What is it about marriage that intrigues you so?"

"I should think it shall be fun to be married before Mary and Kitty, for they are older than I am. I should have a good laugh at them were I married first."

"Ah, is there anything else about marriage that you look forward to?"

"La! Other than marrying before my older sisters, what else is there?"

"I would ask you to take a moment to think about it."

Lydia placed her finger to her cheek and contemplated what she would say next. "I suppose being mistress of my own home and having my own servants and my own pin money will be a good thing, but I never really think about such matters."

"When I have thought of marriage, the thing I consider most is what takes place intimately between a man and his wife. Although, I do not ever suppose I would marry someone if I did not know in advance what to expect in that regard. I trust you understand what I am saying."

Lydia pursed her lips in a rare moment of reflection. "No, I have not the slightest idea."

"What I am saying is, before I marry I expect my bride to give herself to me—before we exchange vows."

Covering her mouth with her hand, she looked around to make certain no one else in the room was privy to their conversation. "Mr. Wickham, I have never heard such a thing, and I have always been taught to know that a bride must wait until after the wedding to consider such a thing, and then she must find it terribly unpleasant, else her husband will think she is wanton."

"I am not surprised that you would have been taught that, but I am … shall I say … rather well-proportioned, and I should like to know in advance that everything fits my bride—it is essential if I am to make the right choice, for I believe strongly in the notion of there being one woman for one man; however, it must be the right woman in every way."

"It sounds as if you are saying that a woman does not stand a chance of being your wife unless you … unless she—"

"That is exactly what I am saying." After glancing about the room, Wickham took Lydia's hand in his and kissed the inside of her palm. "While it is true that you have stolen my heart, I will need something far more meaningful—a confirmation, if you will, before I can entertain the notion of our being man and wife." He smoothed his thumb against the back of her hand, before releasing it. "You would like me to consider making you my wife, would you not?"

"Oh, Wickham, you know I would."

"Then you now know what you must do to help me along."

Lydia did not know what to make of the dashing officer standing before her. He was offering her the key to his heart, and all she needed to do was prevail upon herself to accept it. She closed her eyes and tried to imagine how it would be, but she had nothing with which to measure the prospect. His mention of being *well-proportioned* conjured images of the horses in her father's stable. She opened her eyes, stole a peep at the shiny buttons on his jacket, and then allowed her eyes to wander free—lower and lower still. There was something there, but nothing like the horses. Perhaps it would not be too bad, and she really, really wanted to be married. She gazed up into his eyes and saw something she had never seen before. Indeed, his piercing gaze bore all the best markings of love.

She placed her hand on her ample bosom. "I do want to be your wife, and I am willing to do anything to prove it."

"Are you certain of this?"

"I am positively certain. I should not imagine anything better than being called Mrs. Lydia Wickham."

He leaned a bit closer and lowered his voice. "Can you get away from the house at morning's first light?"

"Oh, no! I never rise as early as that!"

He drew a frustrated breath and then quickly recovered his former attitude. "It seems you are not ready after all. Oh, well … will you pardon me, Miss Lydia."

Lydia grabbed hold of his arm. "I suppose I can make an exception, for, as I said, I would do anything for you."

He shook his arm free. "Indeed. Then we shall meet first thing in the morning." Speaking in hushed tones once more, Wickham told her the precise time and place to meet him. He calmed her uncertainties with sweet assurances that he would be there waiting for her, eager to embark upon their new adventure—together. "Mind you, you are to tell no one what you are about. This must be our particular secret."

Wickham walked away with his head full of the notion that he would have that silly girl whimpering in his arms in a matter of hours. He was no stranger to the flesh, but it was not often that he took a virgin. At least, he hoped she was a virgin, but even if she were not, she was supposed to be a gently bred woman. She would serve as a pleasurable distraction while he wooed Georgiana Darcy.

A connoisseur of carnal pleasures, he had taken his fill of servants, and bedding one of Darcy's sisters while wooing the other was in every way fitting, in Wickham's opinion. Of course, he did not actually plan to share a bed with the girl. Visions of taking her on the bare ground, against a tree, or sprawled over a bale of hay all came to mind. George Wickham's manhood was practically dancing, and he knew that if he did not steal away to the coolness of the fresh night air, he might embarrass himself, such was his desperate need of relief.

Perhaps, he would take a servant—just for the night. Fifteen minutes in a dark corner was all that it would take, and he had just the woman in mind. She even looked like Lydia Bennet with her long, dark hair, and her womanly curves: generous hips and rounded breasts. Were it not for his urgent desire to feast upon those luscious offerings, he would surely take her from behind and pretend he was having his way with Lydia. The way Lydia had flaunted her breasts in his face that evening had almost been his undoing with her low cut décolletage leaving little to his imagination. Did she even know what she did to him?

Thoughts of the morning to come accompanied George Wickham as he quietly escaped the room and made his way to the back of the manor house. He hoped he would see Sally, and after a quarter hour spent lurking about in the shadows, he did. It was indeed his lucky night for she knew exactly what he was about. She required no wooing at all. She nearly raced into his arms. He steered her to an empty storage room. Immediately, he pulled down her chemise and buried his head in her ample bosom. With her, he could do things that his first time with the Bennet girl would never allow. No, it might take at least a week before he could do to her what he planned to do with Sally.

Her soft moans recalled him to his purpose. She needed her release just as much as he needed his, for that is what kept the likes of her coming back—wanting, needing, beseeching. Soon, Lydia Bennet would be begging him for more too.

Chapter 16

Ben stood at the window of his medieval fortress, his spyglass to his eye, keeping faithful watch over the king's land, when he noticed a splash of red moving steadily along the lane and then darting into the woods. He soon supposed it was an officer from the militia. That was something worth investigating, but he remembered Darcy's admonishment to keep his distance from the militia.

On the other hand, as a good watchman, he felt obliged to investigate what was going on. He was about to pack his things and scuttle down to the ground when someone else came into view. A fair lady skipped along the path. Closer scrutiny revealed this was no fair lady at all. It was Aunt Lydia, and she was alone. He was no stranger to her wont of walking to Meryton nearly every day, but never had he known her to walk anywhere unaccompanied and especially not this early in the morning. *Where is Aunt Kitty?* Ben's interest was piqued when he observed his aunt Lydia veer off the main path in the same direction as the officer he had espied earlier.

He imagined the militia must be conducting some secret mission and perhaps his aunt Lydia had been taken into their confidence. *Perhaps she is a spy acting in service of the kingdom!*

Ben suspected that Darcy did not care very much for Lydia, for he rarely, if ever, spoke to her more than was necessary in greeting or farewell. More telling was the absence of warmth in his demeanour when he was with Aunt Lydia that always existed when he was with Aunt Georgiana. Surely this intelligence would increase his esteem, for who did not admire a spy sacrificing herself on behalf of her country?

No—I dare not breathe a word of any of this to a single living soul, for doing so would surely brand me a traitor to my country.

Besides, Ben had another purpose in being out and about so early that morning. His mama had pointed out the road to his dearly beloved Grandfather Carlton's estate the other day, and Ben was determined to journey there on his own. He was not unaware how this would meet with his mama's objections, what with her having said on more than one occasion that she did not approve of the people who now resided at Camberworth. Ben had no intention of seeing any of them. He simply wanted to return to the place that belonged to his late father's father. If he were quick about it, he would return to his fortress by early afternoon, and no one need ever know about his adventure.

Later that day, Darcy and Bingley nearly collided in the doorway of Bingley's study. Bingley stepped aside. "I say, old man, where are you headed in such a hurry?"

"I must be off to retrieve my son."

"Did you not say your London solicitors were due to arrive within the hour? What of your meeting?"

Without pausing for even a second, Darcy said, "Tell them to await my return."

Ever since Ben had wandered off from Cheapside that harrowing day last spring, Darcy had made certain Ben was properly escorted wherever he went. Having no reason to suppose Ben would venture beyond the confines of the Longbourn estate, Darcy had relaxed his restrictions in Hertfordshire. Now learning what a mistake that had been, he did not know whether to be aggrieved or amazed upon receiving word of Ben's whereabouts that afternoon.

Upon being announced, Darcy strode into the room. Ben pushed his chair away from the small table where he and his uncle Henry Carlton sat and rushed to Darcy's side. Carlton, a tall gentleman with dark hair and a slender build, was right behind his nephew. The gentlemen bowed.

"Mr. Darcy, it is a pleasure to see you again."

"Indeed."

Ben's eyes opened wide. "You already know my father, Uncle Carlton?"

"Indeed, your father and I had the pleasure of making each other's acquaintance when he first arrived in Hertfordshire."

A servant entered the room, and Carlton excused himself, thus allowing Darcy and Ben a bit of privacy.

"Why did you keep your plans to visit Camberworth a secret?"

"I am sorry. I should have told you, for I knew you would understand, but you would have told Mama."

"Why should your mother be kept in the dark?"

Ben lowered his voice to a whisper. "Mama does not like the people who reside here."

"I will have to inform her, for there are no secrets between your mother and me."

Carlton approached Darcy and Ben. "You know, I truly do not mind that my nephew thought to come all this way to visit. I was delighted to renew our acquaintance, for he was so very young when we last saw each other."

He turned to Ben. "If your parents will allow it, you are invited to return at any time during your stay in Hertfordshire. In fact, if Mr. Darcy is agreeable, I would love for the two of you to join me for a day of fishing. What say you, Mr. Darcy?"

"I see no harm in that."

"Capital!"

Taking his son by the hand, Darcy said, "Ben, we must be off, for I have a prior engagement this afternoon. I can delay it no longer. Say goodbye to your uncle."

Shortly thereafter, Darcy and Ben sat high upon Darcy's stallion, which trotted along at a slow, steady pace. Ben's pony trailed behind them. Darcy said, "Ben, although your mother and I strongly believe in the importance of familial legacy, that does not give you licence to discover it on your own. You were wrong to wander off to Camberworth all alone. Your act will not go unpunished. You do understand, I pray."

His lower lip trembling, Ben turned to face Darcy. "I hope you are not saying I cannot return to Camberworth. Pray you and I will go fishing with my uncle."

"I gave my word that we shall return to go fishing. I shall not disappoint you in that. I believe family is important, and you ought to know your father's family as well as you know the Bennets and the Fitzwilliams."

"When shall I meet my Darcy relatives?"

"I am afraid that, aside from an uncle who lives on the continent, we have no other known relatives on my father's side of the family."

"I should very much like to meet him." An air of enthusiasm spurred him on. "When we meet, shall I call him Uncle Darcy or Mr. Darcy?"

"I suppose you might call him either of the two. It depends upon what makes you comfortable."

Ben turned and smoothed his hand on the stallion's dark, shiny coat. "What of his friends? Do they call him Darcy?"

"I imagine they might. Why do you ask?"

"Well, my uncle said his friends call him Carlton. He said when I grow up all my friends will call me Carlton too."

"That is true."

His voice riddled with curiosity, Ben said, "How will we know which of the two of us is being talked about when we are together?"

"You will know."

"I like my uncle very much. I think he and I will be great friends." Ben nestled closer and turned to face Darcy again. "But you need not worry."

"Oh?"

"Indeed. Even though you are my father, you will always be my best friend."

"I was of the opinion Samuel had claimed that spot."

"Oh, but it is very different."

"How so—if I may ask?"

Ben raised his finger to his lip. "Allow me to think." After a moment he said, "If I could never see anyone in the world ever again but one, save my mama, I would want to see you."

Darcy placed a kiss atop Ben's head. "I feel the exact same way, my son."

* * *

Elizabeth placed her fingers under her son's chin and lifted his face. "I understand you enjoyed quite an adventure this afternoon, young man."

"Oh, yes, Mama. Although, I know I should never have gone all the way to Camberworth on my own, I simply had to see if it was at all like I remembered."

"May I trust you will never do anything like that again?"

"That I cannot say, for my uncle Carlton has invited Da and me to return."

Elizabeth looked at Darcy, her eyes questioning.

Darcy placed his hands atop Ben's shoulders. "Yes. While exploring the grounds, Ben happened upon a gardener who recognised him. Soon enough, Ben's presence had garnered the attention of most of Camberworth's servants and, ultimately, Mr. Carlton. Ben and his uncle were embroiled in a battle of chess by the time I arrived to claim him."

Ben said, "Indeed. And I was sure that I would emerge the victor, but we ran out of time. And do you know what Uncle Carlton did, Mama?"

"I have not the faintest idea, son. You will have to tell me what your uncle did."

"He left all the pieces standing so that when I return we can pick up our battle exactly where we left off. He said that is how he and his father—my grandfather—left off all their games."

"I am glad you enjoyed meeting your uncle, Ben."

"He is a very kind gentleman. Did you know that Da and my uncle already knew each other?"

Darcy said, "I am afraid Ben suffered a bit of disappointment that he did not have the honour of introducing us."

"Oh, just a little," said Ben. "Although I should like to know how you know my uncle."

Elizabeth said, "I am afraid it is a long story—one I am sure your father will share with you. Only now is not the time, for I need you to prepare for dinner and you know all that entails—especially after an adventure the likes of which you enjoyed today."

Once Ben had quit the room, Elizabeth turned to Darcy. "It sounds as though Ben had quite a day at Camberworth. In spite of that, do you suppose it is wise for him to make a habit of visiting there?"

"Although I was as dismayed as you that Ben made his way so far on his own, I suppose if he must return to the place that means so much to him because of its familial ties, so long as I am with him, no harm will result."

"I take it you have said nothing to Ben about your favourite wish that Camberworth will one day be his."

"No—until I have a firm commitment from Carlton, I shall not raise Ben's hopes in that regard."

"At least there is something we can agree on regarding this whole business scheme. May I ask if you are having any luck in persuading Mr. Carlton to your purposes?"

"No—not yet."

Despite Darcy's reassurances, Elizabeth's misgivings would not be repressed.

"I do not know that I am entirely comfortable with Ben's becoming attached to his uncle. There is a reason, after all, why I did not deem Camberworth a proper environment for my son once his uncle took over as master."

"I assure you the situation now is not at all as it was."

"Still, this situation is fraught with disappointment. I should hate to contemplate Ben's heartbreak should his hopes be shattered."

"Should something like that unfold, we shall both be here for our son." Darcy took Elizabeth's hand in his. "That being said, do you think there is a chance in the world that I would take Ben there if I thought anything of the sort might occur?"

"Anything can happen."

"Ben ought to know his only adult uncle."

"What if Ben's relationship with his uncle fares no better than your relationship with his lordship?"

"Actually, I was exceedingly fond of my uncle when I was young. It was only after he ascended to the earldom that we began to grow apart. I suppose he took his role as head of the family a bit too far," Darcy said in reference to the lengths to which the Earl of Matlock had gone for so many years to bring about a union between Darcy and his cousin Anne.

"By his own admission, Carlton is more than agreeable to the scheme. He looks forward to getting better acquainted with Ben. Besides, how many times have you said that Ben ought to know all of his relations?"

"Must I remind you of the reason I left Camberworth in the first place?"

"I recall your saying how the widow Carlton had created such an unsavoury environment that you thought it unwise to allow Ben to be raised there. Well, it appears that Carlton now shares your sentiments. I have it on good authority he has put an end to all that. He went as far as to relegate the widow Carlton and her child—his stepbrother—to the dowager house, a situation that she found unbearable, and, as a result, she retired to Bath with her child."

"And you know this because?"

"As I am intent upon procuring the estate for Ben, my solicitors are well-versed on any and every matter that might affect my purpose."

"Supposing such a thing is even possible," said Elizabeth.

"It is Ben's legacy. I am obligated to try; it is the least I can do. While Ben is not the heir to Pemberley, he will have his place as my eldest son. I want him to have the certainty of knowing that, when he is of age, he will immediately take his place amongst the landed gentry. What better way than to be master of his own estate; specifically, the Carlton family estate?"

Elizabeth said, "I can see you are determined to arrange every aspect of Ben's future."

"I do not deny that I would do anything in my power to see that Ben does not suffer one bit as he takes his rightful place in society. It simply would not do to have someone whose fortune is as great as Ben's be without an estate grounded by his own roots."

"Do you mean to say, like Mr. Bingley?"

"Yes—in a manner of speaking. Bingley's coming into a substantial fortune and haphazardly settling upon a suitable estate is not something I would wish for our son and neither should you. Ben should not suffer a single moment of not knowing who he is or where he belongs and, as long as it is within my power, he will not."

Chapter 17

A week later found Lydia and Wickham in what was by now their special place—tucked away just off a wooded path. The bliss of their early morning tryst having faded was evidenced by Lydia's pouting lips. Her arms crossed over her bosom, she sang an all too familiar tune in Wickham's ear.

"I am no fool. I know you like her, else you would not spend time walking about in the garden with her when she visits Longbourn. Why bother with her at all?"

Enough! Standing and securing his trousers, Wickham said, "The truth is, Lydia, I have been giving a bit of thought to the situation between Miss Darcy and me. I know precisely what it looks like. You must understand that I need to marry a woman of fortune in order to attain my desired style of living. I do not always intend to remain in the militia. That is the reason I have been spending time in her company. She is very rich, and she and I share a history."

"La! You know how much I want to get married, and you promised me that once you were certain I would make a proper wife, you would marry me. I insist upon being satisfied."

"And you shall be, if you will but hear me out. How should you like to be mistress of Netherfield Park?"

Although attempting to cover her bosom, she scampered to her knees. "Oh! Wickham, do you mean to say you plan to purchase Netherfield Park for me? I declare, I shall go distracted."

"No, I do not have the means of buying such an estate. No—you shall set your cap on Charles Bingley, and I shall set mine on Miss Darcy, and we will both be rich. Then, as we shall all be family, we can always be in each other's company, and only you and I will know and understand how much we love each other. Once you have satisfied your obligation to beget Bingley's heir, you shall return to my bed. The best part is we shall have all the things we desire, and no one will be the wiser."

Lowering himself to his knees, he bestowed a lingering kiss upon her swollen lips and then assisted her in righting her gown. "Because you and Miss Darcy are family, you and I shall have the best of both worlds, for we shall always have the means of being together," he trailed his fingers along her cheek and brushed a light kiss upon her lips, "like this."

He pulled her into his arms. "Surely you see the genius in my plan."

She nodded.

"I knew you would, for you are such a clever girl. I mean to reward you for your understanding. Meet me tomorrow. After I have thanked you properly, I shall tell you what you must do to carry forth our scheme."

"Oh! Wickham, I dare say you are far cleverer than I shall ever hope to be. While I do not know how I shall like being Mrs. Bingley, I do so like Netherfield Park and the delicious idea of being its mistress. And won't we have a good laugh as we both are marrying someone else when we know in our hearts that we belong to each other?"

* * *

All Lydia's efforts to persuade her sister Elizabeth to invite the Longbourn party to dine at Netherfield had been in vain. Elizabeth had insisted it was not her place to prevail upon Bingley's hospitality in that way. How was Lydia to carry out her scheme in the face of such opposition? Bingley's sister, Caroline, then joined the Netherfield party, and as Miss Bingley was by no means unwilling to preside at his table, Lydia prevailed upon him directly to host a dinner party just as she had persuaded him once before to give a ball with equal success.

After dinner, when the gentlemen had joined the ladies in the drawing room, the card-tables were placed. Mrs. Bennet, Colonel Fitzwilliam, and Mr. and Mrs. Collins sat down to quadrille; and as Miss Anne de Bourgh chose to play at cassino, Mary and Kitty had the honour of assisting Miss Caroline Bingley to make up her party. This left Elizabeth with the tiresome task of playing with her sister Lydia, all the while attempting to encourage in the latter some modicum of decorum. Bingley and Georgiana rounded out the game.

Darcy was the happy person whose unengaged standing allowed him to sit and read his book at leisure.

The mood at the first table was jovial, owing to the colonel's amiable nature and Mrs. Bennet's animated spirits. The mood at Elizabeth's table was also lively, but not in a happy sort of manner. Lydia could be quite tiresome when she wanted to be, and that evening it seemed to be her fondest wish.

The attitude at Anne's table, however, was rather subdued. Miss Bingley looked as though she would rather be anywhere on Earth but Hertfordshire. Mary, when she was not relating some anecdote on virtuousness, was intent upon winning the game. Kitty did not say much. Her attention was drawn by the goings-on at all the other tables. Not that Anne was one to find fault, for her cousin Richard's scarcely concealed admiration of the beautiful Mrs. Jane Collins held her attention captive.

By now, Anne had abandoned her quest to garner Colonel Fitzwilliam's favour. What was the point? He only looked at her through the eyes of a cousin, a trusted friend at best, but never through the eyes of a lover. With no one in Hertfordshire urging her along—namely her mother and her dear uncle, Lord Matlock—she simply taught herself to accept that she and Richard would never be more than friends. Thoughts of being of service to her friend persuaded her to approach him in the drawing room after dinner.

Anne cleared her throat. "If you are hoping for a chance to garner Jane's affections, you had better get in line."

"I beg your pardon?"

"Well, look at her. She is happy with her husband and, perchance she is not, she has Charles Bingley waiting in the wings."

"Charles Bingley?"

"Of course, do you claim not to see how much he adores her?"

"Anne, as much as I respect you, I would have to say that you know not of what you speak."

"As regards Bingley's sentiments, cousin, or yours?"

"Why, mine, of course. I dare not speak for another. That being said, what you are positing is not exactly the sort of thing a single woman ought to be discussing with a gentleman."

"What you are saying is fair enough, cousin. Pardon me for speaking out of turn. I will, however, leave you with this." Anne leaned closer. "What you have no doubt been contemplating since your arrival in Hertfordshire is not the manner of behaviour befitting a *true* gentleman."

✳ ✳ ✳

Certain that Charles Bingley was in hearing distance, Lydia set her scheme into motion. "Lizzy, I fear there may have been something in tonight's meal that disagrees with me. I feel very ill."

Elizabeth reached her hand out and placed it on her sister's arm. "This is dreadful news. Shall I summon a carriage to return you to Longbourn? That way the rest of the party may continue to enjoy the evening."

"How I wish that was the thing to do, for I can hardly countenance being the cause of denying anyone's pleasure. However, I feel far too wretched to even consider travelling by carriage." She hugged her stomach. "Why, the very idea makes me nauseous."

His face riddled with concern, Bingley drew closer. "Pardon me, ladies, but I could not help overhearing just now that you are feeling poorly, Miss Lydia. I shall not hear of your leaving. You must stay here at Netherfield until you are fully recovered."

"Oh! No—Mr. Bingley. I should never dream of imposing upon your generosity in such a manner," Lydia protested rather weakly.

"It shall be no imposition at all. We have more than enough room. I say it is the thing to do, especially as you suspect there may have been something about the meal that disagrees with you. It is my obligation to see to your comfort." He placed his hand on Lydia's arm. After glancing about the room, he returned his attention to her. "I do not see Caroline. I shall speak with my housekeeper myself in order that she might make arrangements for your stay."

"You are very kind, sir. Do ask your housekeeper to place me in an apartment close to my dear sister Lizzy, for I am not at all comfortable with the notion of being separated from my family, even for a single evening. I shall find it most comforting knowing Lizzy is nearby."

"Indeed, Miss Lydia. I comprehend your meaning perfectly, and I shall make certain my housekeeper is aware of your concerns."

When Bingley was gone, Elizabeth crossed her arms. "Lydia, I suppose you are pleased with yourself."

"Pleased, Lizzy? How might I possibly be pleased? I feel positively wretched."

"If you insist." Taking her sister by the arm, Elizabeth led Lydia to the chair closest to the parlour door. "Have a seat and wait here for Bingley's housekeeper. I shall inform Mama that you will be staying the night."

Elizabeth walked away, a gnawing sense of trepidation nipping at her heels. Oh, how her mother would delight in the idea of Lydia spending the night at Netherfield. Bingley was, after all, a single man with a large fortune and, if she knew her mother at all, her fondest wish for that evening would be that Bingley might take a second look at one of her unwed daughters. With Lydia being her favourite, Elizabeth suspected her mother's reaction upon hearing the news would be perceived as more vulgar than concerned for Lydia's well-being, assuming she truly was ill.

Moments later, Lydia followed the housekeeper up the stairs. When they were headed down the corridor of apartments, Lydia commenced the next part of her scheme. "As I told Mr. Bingley, the thought of being away from Longbourn for even one night is discomforting to me. If it is not too much trouble, would you tell me who is the occupant of each of these rooms in the event I awaken during the night and lose my bearings should I happen outside my apartment in search of my dear sister? I should hate very much to find myself out of place. Mr. Bingley did tell you that I wanted to be close to my sister, did he not?"

"Yes, ma'am. I believe you will find the room very much to your liking."

"Which of these rooms belongs to Mr. Bingley?"

"That would be the room just up the corridor to our right."

Looking ahead, Lydia counted at least four doors on the right. "I see more than one door. To which do you refer?"

"It is the third door, ma'am."

Lydia had not noticed that the housekeeper was standing still. The elderly woman cleared her throat, garnering Lydia's attention. "This is your room. Mrs. Darcy's apartment is two doors down on the left, ma'am."

Soon after the housekeeper had quit the room with assurances that a maid would arrive shortly to attend Lydia's toilette, Lydia raced to the bed and landed upon it with a gleeful thump. *That was so much easier than I ever supposed.*

My Wickham shall be so pleased. She rolled on her stomach and cupped her hands about her chin. *Now, if carrying out the second and most important part of my scheme should prove half as easy as this, I shall be mistress of Netherfield Park in no time at all, for I shall insist upon a quick wedding.* Lydia pursed her lips. *I wonder if we might be married by special license.*

✽ ✽ ✽

Darcy and the colonel stood opposite each other in the billiards room after the Longbourn guests had departed and most of the household had retired.

"You and Anne seem to have grown closer since Kent."

Richard said nothing as he contemplated his next shot. Once he was positioned to sink the ball in the corner pocket, he said, "Methinks the gentleman sees that which he wishes to see." A knowing expression then accompanied a successful shot.

Slightly impressed with his cousin's proficiency, Darcy studied the table in preparation for his turn. "On the contrary. I saw the two of you speaking rather intimately earlier this evening."

"Actually, our dear cousin was admonishing me for what she perceived as interest on my part in the stunningly beautiful Mrs. Collins."

"Pray you have done nothing to act upon your *interest*."

"As of yet—no."

"Hear me when I say this, cousin. You are not the friend I always supposed you were if you would seriously consider behaving in a manner that forces me to align myself with Geoffrey Collins."

Richard huffed. "You feel that strongly about it then?"

"Is it not what I have been saying all along?" Darcy readied himself to take his next shot. "For heaven's sake, Jane is my sister. I will not stand by idly and watch anyone cause her harm, and that includes you."

"Fear not, my friend. If I did not realise it before, I certainly know now that Mrs. Collins is indeed satisfied with her husband. She is safe from me."

"That is all I want to hear."

"Somehow, I rather doubt that."

"Well, there is one other thing. I would rather suppose your newly established stance increases the possibility of your consideration of Anne."

"I promise you this, old fellow. If my feelings for our cousin develop into the kind of ardent affection she deserves from a husband, you shall be the second to know."

"You mean second to Anne, of course. I would expect no more."

"On the contrary—I meant second to my father."

* * *

Lydia did not get a minute of sleep, having paced the floor for what seemed an eternity, waiting for everyone in the household to settle into their beds and their ensuing deep slumber. At around two o'clock, she donned the robe the maid had provided, stole up the corridor, and slipped into Bingley's room.

She tiptoed across the carpet to allow for a close inspection just to make certain he was sound asleep. His steady breathing and soft snores told her he was beyond being easily awakened. She had never been inside a single gentleman's apartment before. How different it was from anything she had imagined. She began to wonder about his sleeping attire, among other equally pertinent matters. If she were to marry this man, she might as well know what she was in for. *Wickham said that sort of thing was important, did he not?*

My dearest Wickham has never once allowed me a tiny glimpse, and there is no reason in the world he should have not, for there have been many splendid opportunities. How I should love to know what all the fuss is about.

Curiosity spurred her on. Mindful of what a disaster it would be if she woke him, Lydia slowly drew back the bedcover. Her mouth formed a perfect circle. Her time with Wickham had not prepared her for what she espied.

Thank heavens Bingley was properly attired; however, the part of his nightshirt that held her fixated was better described as a tent—a rather large tent. She slapped her hand over her mouth to keep from gushing aloud. She dropped the cover and tiptoed to the other side of the bed. Her Wickham had instructed her to climb into Bingley's bed and snuggle next to him, but she could not bring herself to do so. After carrying out Wickham's other instructions, she eased over to a comfortable chair. With her arms hugging her knees against her breast, she waited and waited, for hours, until finally she heard stirring in the hallway.

When she was certain the voice outside the door belonged to her brother Darcy, Lydia ruffled her hair, rushed across the floor, and threw open the door. Pleased beyond pleased, her eyes met Mr. Darcy's. What was more, he was not alone.

Chapter 18

Lydia just stood there with her mouth agape. Remembering herself, she crossed her arms over her bosom as if attempting to protect her modesty.

"What is the meaning of this, young lady?"

Lydia said nothing.

After commanding the servant who stood across from him to be on his way, Darcy glared at Lydia. "Step aside." He stormed into the room and saw his friend asleep in bed. Evidence of their assignation, in the form of Lydia's robe, was casually strewn at the foot of Bingley's bed. "Bingley! Wake up!" Darcy's commanding voice drew Bingley from a deep slumber and forced him upright.

His eyes half opened, Bingley said, "What in heavens? Darcy, what has got into you? Is the house on fire?"

Darcy ran his fingers through his hair. "I shall ask the questions here. What has got into you?"

Bingley's faced twisted into a half awakened grimace.

"Miss Lydia just came from your apartment—in quite a state, I might add." Darcy looked over his shoulder and noticed she was still standing there. He did not know whether to be angrier at his friend for taking advantage of the wild child or the young woman herself, whom he always suspected only needed the slightest bit of encouragement to find herself in such a predicament. He picked up the robe and tossed it to her. "Cover yourself, young woman."

Bingley looked at her too—his eyes filled with questions. "Miss Lydia?"

Darcy shook his head. "Is that how it is, Charles? Do you dare pretend to be just as shocked by her being here as I am disgusted to find her here?"

"Darcy, what are you accusing me of?"

His chest tight, his fist clenched at his sides, Darcy's voice hardened. "Is it not obvious, man?"

"I know how it must look to find the young woman here, but I fear there has been some sort of misunderstanding." Bingley threw back the covers and hopped out of bed. He walked barefoot to Lydia and reached out to her, stopping short of touching her arm. "Miss Lydia, you must tell me why you are in my apartment?"

Lydia flung her arms around his neck. "Oh, Charles! What is the point in protesting? We have been found out. I meant to return to my room before the house began to stir, just as you told me I must do, but Darcy saw me in the hallway."

He grabbed her arms and attempted to remove them from his person. "What are you saying?"

"Charles, how can you pretend last night did not happen? You came into my room and looked in on me. I told you that I could not sleep, for I was not accustomed to sleeping in such a great big room all alone. You offered to stay the night with me—to attend to my comfort, and after a while, you persuaded me to join you in your bed, saying that I would rest more comfortably in here."

He shook his head. "Darcy, I have no recollection of any of that ever happening. Miss Lydia, why are you suggesting such a thing?"

"La!" Lydia crossed the room and pulled back the covers; thus revealing the evidence of their nocturnal adventure. "Does seeing this refresh your memory?"

What Darcy and Bingley saw marring Bingley's otherwise pristine white sheet left both gentlemen's heads reeling. Bloodstains!

* * *

Later that morning, Lydia pranced into the room, eager to share her happy news. "Oh, Kitty! You will never ever believe my good luck. Mama will be so very pleased when she finds out."

The young ladies clasped hands with each other. "You must tell me at once, Lydia!"

Mary entered the room. "What manner of good luck do you speak of, Lydia?"

Lydia's face twisted with vexation. "Mary, wherever did you come from? I meant for my happy news to be a secret between Kitty and me."

Kitty said, "Oh, Lydia, do not keep me in suspense. I am sure our sister can be depended upon to keep a secret."

"Very well, but I shall only say that soon I shall no longer be residing here at Longbourn, for I shall soon be rich and the mistress of my own home."

Mary's mouth fell open. "Rich *and* the mistress of your own home? Surely you speak in jest!"

"I speak nothing but the truth."

"Who would have asked you to marry him?"

"Mary, how unfeeling you are. Do you mean to say that you find me incapable of landing a rich husband? After all, I am the tallest of all my sisters and the prettiest, and I have more than my share of gentlemen callers."

"And not a rich one amongst them, as best I can tell."

"Oh, Lydia, pay no attention to Mary. Pray tell me, who has asked you to be his wife, and when did it happen?"

"Well—that is the thing. The gentleman has not asked me to be his wife, at least not in so many words, but it is simply a matter of time, and, when he does, you must be sure to be very happy for me, for it shall be a very good thing. And Kitty, you are welcome to come and live with me." She clasped her hands. "We shall have many fine balls, and we shall invite all the officers. We shall have such fun!"

With that, Lydia skipped out of the room with Kitty trailing close behind her, endeavouring to satisfy her curiosity on when the happy occasion would occur, for it had been much too long since they last attended a grand ball. Mary could do no more than shake her head and owe Lydia's improbable account of riches and grand balls to her sister's overabundance of hope and her undeniable want of sensibility.

✷ ✷ ✷

Bingley paced the floor of his study. After a number of starts and stops, endeavouring to make sense of the morning's chaos, he turned to his friend. "Darcy, you must believe me when I say that I do not have a clue how any of this might have happened."

"Charles, you know that I want to believe you—trust me when I say that. But how does one refute such strong evidence? It is one thing that Lydia was even in your room, for she is untamed and unabashed, and she likely views this matter as a game, but how might one account for the bloodstains?"

"Darcy, I know I am not as experienced with the ladies as I might be for a man of my age, but I would like to think that had I—" He ran his fingers through his unkempt hair. "Had I committed such an act with a young woman, then I would surely have some recollection of it."

"I know not what to say that will bring you any sort of reassurance, Bingley."

"You might advise me on what to do and say to prevent me from having to offer for her. I cannot bear the thought of it! If I might be completely honest, the fact is that I do not even like her."

"If it helps, I will tell you that I believe you in that. I find it highly improbable that you willingly sought her attentions, but I do not know if it will make a difference. If I know the young woman, she will have told everyone whose path she has crossed what happened. No doubt she is making plans for a grand wedding and her future life as the mistress of Netherfield. Then, too, there is the matter of the servant who also saw her emerge from your room this morning."

"Oh, Darcy! This is grave indeed. I had no idea there were others involved. I had hoped it would be my word against hers with you vouching for my side of the story."

"Bingley, it would never be as simple as that, and you know it. Think rationally, man."

"What are you saying, Darcy? Are you saying I have to offer her my hand?"

"I am saying that you will have to do what is expected of you to right this situation."

Bingley sat and covered his face with both hands. "What will Mrs. Collins think when she hears of this?"

"I beg your pardon?"

"Jane. Darcy, you must know what she means to me—how I value her good opinion above all else."

"The better question is what that husband of hers will think. You know he fancies himself the Bennet family's protector in Mr. Bennet's stead. No doubt, he will be eager to see the younger daughter married and away from Longbourn as soon as he learns of this."

* * *

For the first time in her young life, Lydia walked to Meryton alone. She simply could not wait to share the good news with her heart's one true love. Espying him on the street with Mr. Denny, she thought nothing of approaching the officers and beseeching Wickham for a private tête-à-tête. After they had walked only a short distance from where Mr. Denny still stood, Lydia commenced her speech.

"Oh, my dearest Wickham, things went exactly according to plan, just as you said they would."

"That is excellent news; however, I suppose nothing is truly decided. It is rather too soon. You must not say a word about what really happened, else it shall all be for naught."

She threw her hands about his neck. "How clever you were to give me the vial of blood, although I must say it was the most disgusting thing ever. Why, I nearly fainted when I opened the bottle, but I am certain Mr. Darcy and Mr. Bingley would not have believed a word I said had I not shown them the irrefutable proof."

He jerked her hands from his person. "Lydia, how many times must I remind you that we need to keep our mutual love for each other a secret, else neither of us shall reap the fortune we deserve." He tugged at his attire and stood straight and tall. "Now, you mentioned Darcy. Is he the one who bore witness to what occurred?"

"Yes, I thought it would be so much better were he the one to witness me coming out of Mr. Bingley's apartment. Oh, you should have seen his face."

Wickham smirked. "I can well imagine." *This is a far better outcome than I had expected. At the least, he will not attempt to align Georgiana with his idiot best friend.* "Did I not tell you before how clever you are? I can hardly wait to reward you."

She simpered and flashed a coltish smile. "What do you have in mind?"

He looked over his shoulder to make certain no one might overhear. He lowered his voice. "Meet me at our place at dawn."

Lydia batted her eyes. "It shall be my pleasure."

"Another thing, whenever we are in company, you must make a show of talking to some of the other officers, else you might give rise to speculation."

"But I should hate to do anything that would give you cause for jealousy."

"Jealousy—how might that possibly be when you and I know the truth? We are too close to having our fondest wishes come true to jeopardise it all."

Chapter 19

Collins, Jane, and Lydia sat in the library—the former on one side of the desk and the latter two opposite—embroiled in discussion of the rumour that, by now, had made its way to Collins. Confused by all that her sister had accused the honourable Charles Bingley of doing, Jane said, "It seems odd that Mr. Bingley would behave as you suggest, for anyone who knows him would say he is the consummate gentleman. Are you certain everything unfolded just as you said, Lydia? It is not too late to clear up any misunderstanding."

"La! Jane, you are determined to believe that just because Mr. Bingley did not love you as much as you would have liked that he cannot possibly be in love with me."

Collins stared at his wife. "What is she saying?"

"Tell him, Jane. Tell him how everyone in the neighbourhood was certain Mr. Bingley was going to make you an offer of marriage, but he did not. No—he left with nary a word. He did not care enough for you to say goodbye. Now he prefers me, and you are jealous." Lydia poked her tongue at her wounded eldest sister. "So, there!"

Collins stared at the sisters, his face red and his fists gripping the arms of the chair. "I have heard all I will hear from you, young lady. Leave—now! I shall decide what is to be done to salvage this wretched situation."

"What can possibly be wretched about a wedding? Oh, how I adore weddings. And I shall have a lovely wedding trousseau."

Collins bolted from his chair. "Leave!"

Lydia's mouth gaped. It took a moment to fashion an apt response. "You dare speak to me in that tone, when I shall be so very rich and all you have to look forward to is this old place."

He looked as if he were about to jump over the desk to rid himself of Lydia's presence. Standing, she said, "Oh, I shall leave. And fear not, Jane, for I shall be certain to invite you and your husband to all my fine balls, even if he is so very unpleasant."

Jane stood to take her leave soon after Lydia quit the room. Collins had other ideas.

"Is there any truth at all to what she said—about Bingley and you?"

"I am afraid her assertions are not without cause."

He released a disgusted breath. "I suppose that explains a great deal."

"Now, surely you do not think me jealous of Lydia."

"Do I believe you are jealous because she has trapped that fool? Preposterous!"

Jane did not know that she would describe Bingley in such unflattering terms, but rather than hone in on the affront, she said, "So, you doubt Lydia's version of the story as well?"

"Whether I believe her is of little consequence. The fact of the matter is there is the perception of wrongdoing on Bingley's part. There is only one way to remedy the situation."

Jane approached her husband, who by now was facing away from her and staring out the window.

"He must marry her," said he.

"Earlier, you said Lydia's outburst explains a great deal. Whatever did you mean?"

"It explains why the man looks at you the way he does—with little to no concern whether anyone notices him."

He turned to face her; Jane lowered her eyes. Collins placed his hand under her chin and directed her gaze to meet his. "Surely you are no stranger to the way he feels."

Jane said, "Pray, tell me that what Lydia said about my feelings for Mr. Bingley and what you now suppose as his lingering feelings for me have no bearing on your good opinion of me."

Collins took her hand in his. "No, of course not, my dear, for there is nothing in the world anyone might say to me that would change the way I feel about you—about us. We both have our own past. What is important is what we make of our present and our future—together."

* * *

Darcy and Bingley stood when Mr. Geoffrey Collins stormed into the room. From the looks of him, he was armed for battle.

"Mr. Bingley, it is good of you to see me, but I would, however—" he looked at Darcy and then back at Bingley, "prefer a private audience with you."

"What can you have to say to me that my friend should not be privy to?"

"Surely you can be at no loss to understand why I am here. Gossip of what occurred under this roof is spreading."

Bingley crossed his arms. "I will marry her."

"It is good to know that you are reasonable."

"As I see it, I have no choice, and from this moment on, I shall not speak ill of the woman who is to be my wife."

"Good, I would rather you did not. You will understand there are certain arrangements that must be made, and I will be the one to oversee them in Mr. Bennet's stead."

"I shall leave it to whoever is most interested in that sort of thing to work out the details of the wedding; however, as far as the marriage settlement is concerned, Darcy and I have already hammered an agreement. The details have been dispatched to my solicitor in town. You will find my offer reasonable; however, it is not negotiable."

Collins looked at Darcy. "It seems your friend is well-rehearsed."

"This has nothing to do with me," said Darcy.

"Please—it is always about you."

"The truth is that we all have a stake in this little game, do we not? As we shall all be family, we might as well make the best of it," said Darcy.

"I would hardly say this scandal is merely a game. It is a very serious matter."

"If you knew young Lydia half as well as you think you do, you would know precisely what I mean. But it matters not. The material point is that Bingley has offered to do what is expected of him."

* * *

Later that day, Bingley set off for Longbourn to call on Miss Lydia. How he wished instead that he could summon up the past as he trudged the pathway that led to the Bennets' door. He imagined himself striding along with a spring in his step. He imagined a bright, happy smile on his face as he informed the lady of the manor that he wished to have a private audience with Miss Bennet. He even imagined the words he would say to explain away his lapse in judgement for ever having left her side all those months ago when he was first in Hertfordshire, how he had been a complete and unmitigated fool for not following his heart. How his life had been a torment during their long separation, and how he wished for nothing more than to offer her his hand in marriage. All this he imagined himself uttering on bended knee and gazing up into a pair of the most angelic eyes he had ever seen. He imagined those eyes glistening with tears of joy. Her answer would be yes ... yes, I will marry you, Charles, for there is not another man in the world for me, but you.

Stark reality pierced Bingley's blissful musings as he considered those very words. The harsh fact was that there *was* another man for his Jane: her husband, Geoffrey Collins. Only an act of God would change that. Bingley's heart sank in his chest. *By then it will be too late. I shall be married to her silly sister, Miss Lydia.* His countenance coloured with contrition. *Not that I would wish to see my Jane a widow even for an instant, for she truly deserves the happiness she seems to have found. As for her sister, I must teach myself to stop thinking of her as the witless girl that she is, and I must start to revere her as my future wife.*

Upon entering the paddock and surrendering his horse to a servant, Charles lumbered on with the feeling of this being the longest distance he had ever walked when, in reality, the stairs leading to the front door were but a stone's throw away. Sorrow accompanied those last steps of the way. Here he was, a young man in the prime of his life, suffering feelings akin to losing everything.

Darcy had offered to accompany him in a show of moral support, but Charles had declined, thinking this was something he truly needed to do alone. The truth is he wanted as few people as possible to bear witness to what surely would be a spectacle. *Heaven knows how Mrs. Bennet will carry on.*

Of course, the Bennet household reaction would be nothing in comparison to Caroline's once she learned what he had done—that he had actually offered his hand to Lydia. He recalled how disgusted she had been all those months ago when they first came to Netherfield Park and everyone suffered the general expectation that he was to be married within months to the eldest Bennet daughter. How livid she was after hearing Mrs. Bennet speculate aloud that there was to be a wedding at Netherfield Park in three months. Caroline had been so distraught over the prospect of such an alliance between the two families that she would not rest until they took their leave of Hertfordshire within hours of the ball; the ball he had given at Miss Lydia's request, but as far as he was concerned, in Jane's honour.

By now, Bingley had reached the door. He just stood there, frozen, faced with the certainty that, once he crossed the threshold, life as he knew it would never be the same again. *There is no turning back now.*

Moments later, Bingley was standing in the parlour, his eyes fixed upon Jane and filled with unspoken apology. Without looking away, he swallowed. "Mrs. Bennet, I wish to have a private audience … with Miss Bennet."

"Miss Bennet? You mean to say you wish to have a private audience with Mary?" Her loud, shrieking voice revived his senses.

He shook his head and cleared his throat. Finally, he tore his eyes away from Jane's. "I wish to have a private audience with—" Bingley swallowed hard, "with Miss Lydia."

Mrs. Bennet immediately stood to clear the room of everyone save her favourite daughter and her soon to be son-in-law. The spring in Mrs. Bennet's step was just as he had imagined it would have been had he offered for Jane as he ought to have done. However, it was not Jane who raced to his side and attached herself to his arm. His Jane would never have displayed such a lack of decorum. It was not Jane with whom he would henceforth and forever more be associated or whose name would be mentioned when the book was written on the happiest day of his life, and it was not Jane whom he would take to the marriage bed and make his wife, and the sooner he taught himself to accept those truths, the better it would be for him. The better it would be for the future Mrs. Lydia Bingley, and the better it would be for everyone concerned.

Chapter 20

Caroline's face bore an angry shade of disgust. She threw her linen napkin down and pushed her chair away from the table, sending the attending footman scrambling to assist her. "Charles, how could you?"

Caroline could not believe how her brother had made such a farce of his life. She had hoped he would make good use of having Georgiana Darcy in his home and thus satisfy her greatest wish for an alliance between the two families. Helping them along was her sole reason for leaving London before the end of the Season, her brother's future happiness, and thus her own, was just that important. She knew Darcy felt the same way too regarding an alliance between his best friend and his sister. Indeed, it was but one of the things she and Darcy always had in common. Oh, he would never admit it. In fact, he had gone out of his way to deny Caroline any and everything that might bring her a modicum of pleasure since he met that Eliza Carlton.

"Caroline, I know how much you abhor this situation, but it is of no consequence. Miss Lydia Bennet is to be my wife, and there is nothing to be done about it."

"She will marry you over my dead body."

"I would rather it did not come to that."

Elizabeth and Darcy walked into the room. During the days leading up to this debacle, Caroline had done all she could to remain civil to Elizabeth and even her son, whom Caroline swore she was allergic to when speaking to her lady's maid. The reason for her amiable civility towards Darcy's newfound family was her fervent wish to retain the right of visiting Pemberley. The prospect of that wild Lydia Bennet marrying Charles shattered all Caroline's pretences.

"Darcy, how on earth could you have allowed—nay, encouraged—my brother in this foolhardiness?" Caroline demanded.

Darcy looked at Charles. "So, it is done."

"Yes, I have just come from Longbourn."

Elizabeth walked to Charles's side. "So we are to be brother and sister. I imagine my sister and my mama are very excited and no doubt making wedding plans as we speak."

"I believe they are. I mean to say that is what Miss Lydia said they would do when I took my leave."

Caroline's mouth gaped. "Charles, I will not abide this. This is a travesty for our family. Just think of the irreparable harm to our family should that dim-witted girl arrive in town proclaiming herself as Mrs. Charles Bingley. Our family's reputation as upstanding people amongst society will be ruined."

"Come now, Caroline. I can imagine far worse things than being married to my best friend's sister."

"That young trollop barely warrants the distinction."

Caroline Bingley had gone too far. Elizabeth placed her hands about her waist. "I would ask you to refrain from disparaging my sister, Caroline. By Charles's own doing in offering his hand, she will be your sister as well. If for nothing other than the sake of family harmony, you must endeavour to accept it."

"I shall never countenance such a disgraceful alliance." She glared at her brother. "Better that you had married the elder sister than ... than the silliest one of them all."

Bingley narrowed his eyes. "Well, you and I both know why that did not happen, do we not?"

"And you blame me? You may as well point a finger at your best friend."

Elizabeth looked at Darcy. "What on earth is she saying?"

Darcy made no answer.

Charles said, "In the end it is my own doing. I blame no one but myself for this business."

* * *

When the notion of residing at Netherfield Park during their stay in Hertfordshire was first proposed, Elizabeth had supposed its greatest drawback was the possibility that Caroline Bingley would also be in residence. That vile woman had not changed at all since the time Elizabeth last saw her in London. Surely one would think her propensity to fawn over Mr. Darcy would have diminished once he was no longer a single man in possession of the key to her heart—that being the prospect that she would be the next mistress of Pemberley. Sadly, it had not. *Whatever did she mean when she told her brother that he may as well point a finger at his best friend? Did she mean to suggest that my husband had a role in separating Bingley and Jane?*

Elizabeth had held her tongue while in the Bingleys' company, but now she was alone with her dear husband, and she meant to have answers.

"What did she mean? Is this just another instance of Caroline being Caroline, bent on causing trouble, or is there some basis for her scurrilous declaration?"

Darcy shrugged. "Depending upon one's perspective, one might say it is a little of both."

"What are you saying?"

"Caroline feels strongly that there is basis for what she said. I, however, know that her accusation is baseless."

"Sir, just to be clear that we are of one mind on the matter, are you suggesting that she has reason to suspect you had a part in separating Jane and Bingley all those months ago, of exposing one to the censure of the world for caprice and instability, and the other to its derision for disappointed hopes, and involving them both in misery of the acutest kind?"

"I would not go as far as to say all that."

"What *do* you say?"

"Elizabeth, I would not say I had a hand in separating your sister and my friend."

"Yet you did say Caroline has sufficient cause to believe you did."

"As you can rightfully surmise, Caroline was adamantly opposed to an alliance between her brother and your sister Jane. Charles refused to believe her when she posited that Jane was more interested in his fortune than anything else, and when he sought my opinion on whether I believed that Jane did not care for him—"

"What did you say?"

"I told him the only thing I could tell him in good conscience. Regardless of the ardent feelings of love that he professed towards your sister, never did I detect any such feelings in her towards him."

"So, Caroline is correct. You did separate them."

With assumed tranquillity, Darcy said, "No—I did not. Bingley chose to leave Hertfordshire of his own accord."

"Yet one word of encouragement from you might have been all that was required to persuade him to stay."

"It is all speculation at this point, would you not agree?"

"I am appalled, Mr. Darcy, to know that my sister might have been married to Bingley had you offered him the encouragement he sought from you—the encouragement he needed to offer Jane his hand in marriage."

"Bingley is his own man! And no, I did nothing to encourage him. By the same token, I did nothing to discourage him," said Darcy, in a less tranquil tone.

"Yes, you simply stood by and did nothing when my sister might now be married to the man she truly loved—who truly loved her."

"Who is to say she is not currently married to a man who truly loves her—a man she truly loves in return?"

Elizabeth threw up her hands. "I do not know why any of this comes as a surprise to me. From the moment of our first acquaintance, you made no secret of your disdain for my family."

"You will recall that any disdain I may or may not have felt at the time did not extend towards you."

"And this must be your excuse?"

"No—I am not trying to make excuses. Had I detected any symptom of love in Jane towards Charles, I would have told him so."

"Jane rarely shows her true feelings to anyone!"

"And this must be *your* excuse? Pray tell me, dear wife, if Jane had been as much in love with Bingley as you seem to think she was, then why did she not put forth more of an effort to make him aware of her sentiments, especially as she was living in town? How difficult would it have been for their paths to cross, given her prior acquaintance with his sister?"

"Jane is shy! She would never have put herself in the path of a gentleman who had treated her as Bingley had."

"Then that is indeed her misfortune, assuming what you say is true."

"Surely this indifference you feel towards Jane does not extend towards your friend. He loves her still."

"I am well aware of Bingley's continued devotion towards Jane; however, I cannot allow myself to feel any culpability for his heartache. When Bingley learned that you and I had renewed our acquaintance since parting ways in Hertfordshire, he came to me with unfounded accusations of betrayal."

"Why is it that all accusations against you are proclaimed as unfounded, when all evidence suggests otherwise?"

Darcy folded his arms over his chest. "I did not force Bingley to abandon your sister! He made his own choice. What is more, I told Bingley that Jane was residing in Cheapside with the Gardiners."

Elizabeth coloured. "Bingley knew my sister was in town, and he chose to do nothing about it?"

"To be fair, he later told me that he indeed acted upon the intelligence. He did go to Cheapside to see Jane, but he felt that he was too late. You see, he espied her strolling arm in arm with Mr. Collins. He turned and walked away without approaching them."

"Seeing Jane with Mr. Collins is hardly an excuse for his not making his presence known."

"I would agree, but it was not so simple for Bingley, for it was not just that he saw the woman he loved with another man. He saw the woman he loved looking at another man in much the same way as he remembered her looking at himself."

* * *

Elizabeth breathed in the fresh air. A good long walk from Netherfield to Longbourn was precisely what she needed. Her hours at her father's bedside were taking their toll on her spirits, but she would not complain. Her family needed her.

Crossing field after field at a hurried pace, jumping over stiles and springing over puddles with impatient activity, her frustration towards her husband veered in a different, more fitting, direction. *Oh, that spiteful Caroline Bingley! She is miserable, and she will not be satisfied until everyone around her is equally so.*

She knew exactly what she was doing in pointing a not too subtle finger at Fitzwilliam. She meant to stir up trouble between my husband and me, and she almost succeeded.

Of course he did not form a favourable impression of my family upon first making their acquaintance. What a spectacle her two younger sisters had made of themselves when first they all met at the Meryton assembly—the way they jostled with each other to gain the most advantageous position to garner Mr. Bingley's attention.

Oh, how utterly embarrassing. Her mother had been no better, for her intention of promoting a match between one of her daughters and the handsome and rich and oh so amiable Mr. Bingley was made clear from the start. She had even boasted aloud of an impending marriage at Netherfield within the very near future. Then there was Jane's own behaviour towards the gentleman, which, while far above any manner of reproach, might easily have been perceived as a lack of ardent affection.

Now the worst possible scenario has unfolded right before our eyes. Elizabeth did not believe Lydia's account of the events that led to her future marital felicity as a rich woman with many fine carriages and clothes one bit. But what could she say? What could she do? There was only one way to salvage her family's reputation: Bingley must marry Lydia.

What a shame indeed, after all he has done in forgoing the Season in town and being here to host our large party. Is this the gratitude he is to receive, to be tricked into marriage by someone who cares not one fig for him? Elizabeth shook her head. *I will not continue to dwell on this matter, for to do so will result in my own misery. Mr. Bingley suffers enough misery for all of us, including his pernicious sister.*

Chapter 21

"Da, I am not ready to part with my trophy just yet," Ben said as the servant who accompanied them on their fishing party prepared to return to the manor house with the day's catch. How proud and excited the little fellow was over his conquest.

"I see no harm in your accompanying Mr. Hall—assuming your father does not object," said Carlton.

"May I?"

"Yes, you may. However, you are not to wander off on your own. Agreed?"

Ben readily nodded and then fell in step with the tall, lanky young man who also fondly remembered Ben having once resided at Camberworth. Darcy and Carlton watched until Ben and Mr. Hall were well out of sight.

"Ben loves it here," said Carlton.

"Indeed."

"I cannot help but consider that, were my father alive, Ben would still consider Camberworth his home."

"I find it interesting that you would speak this way, Carlton."

"I say only the truth."

The two strode along in uncomfortable quietness.

After a moment, Carlton broke the silence. "I really must thank you for bringing my nephew here today. Perhaps you and his mother will allow me to spend even more time with him, so he and I might get to know each other."

"I see no reason that will not occur with time. Surely you do not suppose one can establish over the course of a few weeks what normally unfolds over the course of several years."

The gentlemen continued going on in that way, but for Darcy one purpose was clear. After decades of estrangement from the elder Mr. Carlton, Henry Carlton had finally returned to Camberworth reclaiming his birth right. Darcy did not fault him for that. However, Carlton's return also evidenced a kind of neglect that was reflected wherever anyone would look. Darcy's solicitors had unearthed intelligence on Camberworth's solvency. In principle, Carlton was a wealthy landowner, but in reality he was in dire need of funds. If there were a chance in the world that Darcy could acquire the estate, he supposed he would be doing all parties involved a great service.

Darcy said, "You and I have already discussed the fact that there is a provision that allows Camberworth's entail to be broken, given that all living heirs must be agreeable. You ought to know that my solicitors have been in contact with Mrs. Carlton. It seems she is not nearly as concerned with her son's potential birth right as one might expect, what with your being a single man and a relatively young one at that."

"You think you have it all figured out, do you not, Darcy? Well, I have conducted a bit of investigation too. Just as there is no amount of money that would tempt you to part with your dear Pemberley, likewise there is nothing that would tempt me to part with Camberworth. You are wasting your time, for I shall never sell."

Darcy halted his steps, obliging Carlton to do likewise. His voice resolute, Darcy said, "My years of negotiating various affairs of business have taught me a great many things, one of them being—never say never."

Lydia would not be satisfied until she and her family were once again invited to a lavish dinner party at Netherfield. She insisted that, once she became mistress, such affairs would be commonplace. Why wait? Her behaviour was everything mortifying, and no one could be impressed with her, other than Mrs. Bennet, who, as a consequence of Lydia's advantageous alliance, was her former self once more.

Throughout the evening, Mrs. Bennet encouraged her daughter in every way to regard anything that brought her displeasure—be it the meals, the furnishings, even a particular servant—as something to be rectified once Lydia became mistress of Netherfield.

There was no want of discourse once the Netherfield party and the Longbourn guests took their places at dinner—at least, not on Lydia's part. The bride and her mother could not talk fast enough about how things would be once Lydia became mistress. Untamed, unabashed, wild, noisy, and fearless, Lydia personified everything a young woman ought not to be. And such a woman was to be mistress of this place—one of the finest homes in all of Hertfordshire? Everyone who would be embarrassed by the unfolding events was exceedingly so, particularly Jane, who often looked at Elizabeth, and no one was happier than the two eldest sisters when, finally, the meal was over.

Elizabeth was appalled, and Jane was embarrassed, and when they could, they spoke on the matter and how it even came about.

"Lydia has always been outrageous with a tendency to place too much stock in her own significance. Now it seems that years of bad behaviour are to be rewarded with Mr. Bingley's hand." Try as Jane might to hide her dismay, Elizabeth knew her sister too well to suppose she was truly unaffected. "I am sorry, Jane."

"There is no need to apologise to me. If anyone, it is Mr. Bingley who should receive condolences—from all of us."

Elizabeth threw a glance across the room. There Bingley stood with Darcy. Gone was his amiable smile, and in its place was a look of confusion. *That befuddled expression has graced his countenance since the day my husband discovered Lydia emerging from Bingley's apartment.*

"I do believe that is one of the most uncharitable things I have ever heard you say, dearest Jane. It appears that you are just as sceptical of Lydia's account of events as I am."

"In truth, I am. However, I find it hard to believe our sister could even conceive of such a scheme, and it is for that reason alone that I am forced to suspend my belief of everything I know and trust about Charl—Mr. Bingley."

"You were about to refer to the gentleman by his given name. Does that mean—"

"Oh, Lizzy, I know what you are about to say. You are concerned I might harbour a tender regard for Mr. Bingley."

"Do you?"

"I suppose I shall always think of him fondly, for he is indeed the first man I ever recall loving. But that seems like such a long time ago. So much has happened—as you well know. I have come to consider that our lives are more than a series of random outcomes ... all things happen for a reason. The wife of Mr. Collins and the mother of his two daughters is the life I was meant for. Indeed, I am very happy."

Elizabeth smiled and embraced her eldest sister. "I am happy for you." Upon resuming her former attitude, she espied her youngest sister skipping across the floor with Kitty bouncing along right behind her. Rolling her eyes, she said, "I believe I *shall* offer Bingley my condolences."

"Yes," said Jane with a hint of mischief in her voice, "and I shall take the opportunity to do the same with Miss Bingley."

Elizabeth's eyes followed Jane's. Caroline Bingley sat off in the corner, her countenance a mixture of outrage and disgust—a powder keg if you asked Elizabeth. *Heaven help us all*.

* * *

With the end of the evening fast approaching, Bingley had not achieved his single, most important resolve—to speak with Jane. Ever since that harrowing day when he went to Longbourn to offer his hand to Miss Lydia, the thought of what Jane must think of him haunted him. Did she think he did not care for her—that he never cared? Every occasion that found them in company since that day also found them in the company of Geoffrey Collins. Rarely did the man leave

Jane's side, and when he did, he never stayed away very long. Finally, when the carriages were ordered to return the guests to their homes, Mrs. Bennet commanded Collins's attention, thus allowing Bingley the chance he longed for.

As Jane was crossing the room, Bingley placed himself directly in her path. Nervous but determined, he said, "When I learned you were in London … last year … there was nothing more important to me than seeing you. I had to see you."

Jane's angelic eyes registered her confusion. "Oh?"

"I came to see you in Cheapside. You were not alone. I saw you walking with Mr. Collins."

"Why did you not say something?"

"You looked happy." Bingley swallowed hard. "As happy as I ever recalled having seen you."

"Still, sir, you might have made your presence known. I am certain I would have been delighted to see you."

"If I supposed for an instant that it would have made a difference in how things turned out, then I should berate myself for all eternity."

"Sir, I know not what to say."

"Tell me if it would have made a difference. If you had known that I had come to see you in Cheapside as soon as it was made known to me that you were in town, would it have been the means of a different outcome than the one we now endure?"

"Surely you cannot expect me to engage in such conjecture, to raise or diminish hopes, when nothing about our situation is ever likely to change. I am married to Mr. Collins, and you will soon be married to my youngest sister."

"Please," said Bingley, his eyes imploring, "one word from you will silence me on this matter forever."

Geoffrey Collins marched over and stood by his wife's side. "Pray I am not interrupting."

How Bingley wished Jane looked at him the way she looked at Collins. She said, "Oh, no, Mr. Collins. Mr. Bingley was simply wishing me goodnight."

Collins arched his brow. "Allow me to accept your good wishes on both our behalf."

"Indeed, Collins; Mrs. Collins, goodnight."

As tormenting as it was seeing the woman he loved being escorted away, the sight of Miss Lydia Bennet prancing his way, solely at her mother's urgings, rendered him even more dejected. What had he ever done to harvest such misery?

Chapter 22

On more than one occasion, he had noticed Georgiana walking and talking with the lieutenant, whom he now discerned as the officer who met his aunt Lydia to conduct spy business. Ben wondered why Georgiana even tolerated George Wickham. Surely she knew how much her brother did not like him. Should she not be equally as wary of such a man? He shook his head. He was certain he would never understand girls. He had even espied Gillian and Emily pretending they were fair maidens in need of rescuing and making believe the *dashing* lieutenant was their knight in shining armour. Ben had but a few opportunities to observe the officer up close. When he saw how the man leered at his aunt Georgiana and even his aunt Lydia—when he thought no one was watching—Ben considered the officer was more of a troll than a knight.

Ben darted behind the bush when he espied his aunt Lydia just ahead. It was not that he did not wish to see her; rather it was the company she was keeping. Seeing how his aunt's mind was so happily engaged in but one thought of late, that being her pending nuptials, Ben no longer considered she was a spy acting on behalf of her country. No, Ben began to consider that something else was afoot. As soon as Lydia pranced off in the opposite direction from where Ben was hiding, the young fellow made his presence known to her former companion who appeared to be waiting for someone.

"Good day, young man," George Wickham said to Ben.

Ben looked at the tall gentleman. He said nothing.

"I take it you do not remember who I am."

"Oh, I remember you."

"Excellent. Pray how are you enjoying your stay in Hertfordshire?"

Ben said nothing in response.

"I imagine you are missing Pemberley, your new home."

Ben continued to regard the officer with circumspection. Da had told him to keep his distance, and that is what he meant to do. But his curiosity about the man who garnered so much of his father's disapprobation could no longer be repressed.

George Wickham took a seat on a bench and crossed his long legs. "You are a most fortunate young man to live there. Did you know that I once lived there as well? My memories of living at Pemberley are some of the happiest of my life. I yearn to see it again."

"I do not suppose that will be happening," said Ben.

"So, you do talk."

"I was told to keep my distance from you, and that is what I mean to do."

"No doubt Darcy advised you to that effect. You honour him as your father, and you do as he tells you. I would expect no less of you. You must always honour and obey your father."

"I do not need you to tell me that, sir, but I would ask one question of you."

"You may ask me anything you like. My life, you see, is an open book. What would you like to know?"

"What are your intentions towards my aunt Georgiana and my aunt Lydia?"

Wickham cleared his throat. "My intentions?"

"Indeed," said Ben, his hands on his hips.

"What is it that you think you know, child?"

"I know what I know."

Wickham uncrossed his legs and reached into his pocket. When he withdrew his hand, it was clasped tightly. "Come here, Ben, I have something for you to see." He tucked both hands behind his back and then brought them back in front of him. "You enjoy games of chance do you not?"

Ben's curiosity overtook prudence, and he stepped closer. "What is the name of this game?"

"I have something of great value in one of my hands. If you correctly guess which hand, its contents shall be yours."

Ben could not resist. He pointed to Wickham's left hand. Wickham opened his hand and revealed his empty palm.

"Shall we try it again?"

Ben nodded.

The officer put his hands behind his back once more, and then brought them forth again. Ben pointed to the left hand again. Wickham opened his hand and revealed a shiny coin.

"You are very clever young man." Wickham handed the coin to Ben.

Young Ben could not help smiling. Looking over the gentleman's shoulder, he saw his aunt Georgiana heading in their direction. "Shall we have another turn?" Ben asked.

George Wickham said, "Not today; however, if you will keep quiet about what you think you know about your aunts and me, there will be more coins where that one came from—many more. Do we have a deal?" He held out his hand to Ben.

For Georgiana's sake, Ben's mouth gaped. "You mean to bribe me!" Ben kicked George Wickham as hard as he could. He had meant to get away, but the tall man was quicker than Ben supposed.

He grabbed Ben by his shoulders and shook him. "How dare you, you wretched—you spoilt bastard. I should turn you over my knee!"

Georgiana was appalled. She gasped. "Unhand my nephew this instant!"

George Wickham released Ben, who managed to land on his backside. "Georgiana, this is not how it looks."

Ben clutched his body and groaned aloud.

"What did you do to my poor nephew?"

"He is no more a nephew to you than I am a brother to you."

"What a vile and wretched thing to say!"

She fell to her knees, assisted Ben to his feet and took him in her arms. "Oh! Ben, pray that evil man did not harm you."

Young Ben sniffed. Patting her on the back, he looked at George Wickham and grinned. His voice trembling, he said, "I think I shall be all right, Aunt Georgiana."

She held him still. "Thank heavens for that." She stood and took Ben by his hand.

"Georgiana, this is not at all how it appears. That little miscreant provoked me. I am the injured party."

"You are never to address me by my given name again!"

He reached out to her. "Please, hear me out."

She jerked away from him. "Do not touch me. Furthermore, you are to stay away from both of us. Should you ever come anywhere near either of us again, I will know how to act."

Chapter 23

Ben raced into the room—his face filled with anticipation and joy. "Da! While keeping watch from my fortress, I saw Uncle Carlton headed towards Netherfield. Did he come all this way to see me? He promised me he would. I should like to show him my fortress!"

"Ben, about your uncle—"

"Where is he? Perchance I missed him, and he is on his way to find me." Ben hurried towards the door.

"Son, where are you going?"

"If I am quick about it, I may be able to catch up with him."

The thought of his son racing after a man who did not even have the courage to say goodbye to his own nephew before leaving the country, perhaps forever, sent a shiver through Darcy's body. Standing, he crossed the room in long strides. Closing the door, he took Ben by the hand. "Ben, come and sit with me."

Ben slipped his hand away. "But what about my uncle? I like him very much, and I should hate to miss him."

Darcy knelt to Ben's eye level and placed his hands on Ben's shoulders. "What I have to say has to do with your uncle. You see, Ben—"

Ben tore away and ran to the nearest window. "Have I missed him? Did he say when he would come back and see me?"

Darcy started walking towards Ben. "Your uncle is leaving the country. He is headed for the continent."

"The continent—but that is so very far away. Did he say when he is to return?"

Once again by Ben's side, Darcy lowered himself to meet Ben eye to eye once more. "I do not know that he ever plans to return. He did ask me to tell you what a great honour it was for him to make your acquaintance and to tell you goodbye." Although disguise of this kind was Darcy's abhorrence, he felt this situation needed embellishment. "He said he will miss you very much, and he will think of you always during his many travels."

"But he must have written a letter. He would never leave without saying a proper goodbye—" Ben lowered his head, "would he?" In a soft voice reflecting a measure of pain mixed with resignation, Ben said, "I shall never see my uncle Carlton again." After a moment of silence, he accepted Darcy's embrace.

"I am sorry, son."

Darcy could no longer see Ben's face, but everything about his comportment gave Darcy to know that Carlton's act had wounded his son. Picking Ben up, Darcy carried him to the sofa, and then sat and held him close. None of this met with any sort of protest on Ben's part—a further testament to the pain he surely must have been suffering. His liveliness …

his high spirits ... all the excitement so clearly evident just moments earlier was now gone.

Darcy's heart sank right along with Ben's. That someone so young and innocent should suffer the pang of loss at so tender an age was unbearable. His heart screamed at the injustice of it all, and not for the first time in his life, he swore that he would do everything in his power to make amends to his son.

Darcy ran his hand through Ben's unruly curls and drew him even closer to his chest. *He is so young and innocent, trusting and loyal. How could anyone not love such a precious child?* Darcy swallowed hard. *All I ever want to do is love and protect him—to keep him safe from harm. Safe from pain—be it physical as well as emotional.* Darcy's eyes misted. *Now he is hurting and in a way that I have never seen him suffer, for it is from the sting of rejection.*

The manner in which Carlton left without wishing to say goodbye to his nephew, his own flesh and blood, stirred Darcy's ire once more. *I say it is his loss.* Darcy closed his eyes as all of Elizabeth's admonishments about the man raced through his head.

If only I had listened. I fear I have failed our son. He placed a light kiss atop Ben's head. "Never again," Darcy said softly.

The events that had transpired earlier in that room flashed before his eyes—how Carlton had come to see him, offering to sell Camberworth in order that he might return to his former life on the continent unencumbered by a grand, cash-poor, estate and demanding tenants and the like.

It will make no difference at all telling Ben that he will be master of Camberworth when he comes of age. What does that matter to a child? There was only one way of easing the pain of Ben's broken heart—by telling him that he would soon see his uncle Carlton again. *That is the one thing my son needs to hear and the one thing I cannot say.*

"Da?"

"Yes, Ben?" Darcy took Ben's tiny hand in his. He gently squeezed it.

"Is Grandpapa Bennet close to getting better now?"

"I believe he is. The physicians attending him are optimistic, and your mother says each day brings him closer to his former self. He is communicating his needs—even beginning to speak. Would you like to visit him this afternoon?"

"I should like that very much, although my reason for asking if he is getting better has to do with something more."

"Oh?"

"Indeed. I very much would like to go home. When shall we return to Pemberley?"

Chapter 24

Wickham hated that his carefully laid plan to marry the rich young Georgiana Darcy had been thwarted, and by a child no less. It had always been his intention to marry her one day. Then there had been his violent confrontation with Darcy, compelling him to leave Pemberley. How fortunate he had thought himself when they all found themselves in Hertfordshire at the same time: Wickham owing to his being in the militia, and the Darcys owing to Mr. Bennet's illness. Speaking of which, what a shock it had been for him to learn that the proud Fitzwilliam Darcy had married into a family so far beneath him in consequence as to be considered laughable.

How the mighty had fallen! was his first impression upon learning the news. Of course, his own circumstances were nothing to be proud of either. The life of a lowly foot soldier was not the life he was meant to have. He was reared right beside the heir of Pemberley, one of the finest estates in all of

Derbyshire, which was really saying something. His godfather, the elder Mr. Darcy, was one of the richest, most powerful men George Wickham ever had the good fortune of knowing. He made no secret of his favouritism for his godson, so much so that George supposed it would always be that way. As sorry as he was for his benefactor's passing, he was even more aggrieved that there had been no provisions at all for his financial well-being, other than the living, which Wickham did not want.

The paltry sum that Fitzwilliam Darcy had given him in lieu of the living bolstered Wickham's hatred towards his childhood friend. Still, he accepted the money, thinking at the time that it was better than nothing. He desperately needed funds; besides, Darcy had more than enough money. Wickham had been certain that he could always prevail upon his childhood friend later on, for Darcy had never been able to deny him anything. Upon learning that Darcy did indeed possess the ability to refuse him, Wickham's response had been violent.

Wickham had left Pemberley for what many thought would be the last time; however, he never believed it for a second. He had not spent so much time effectively wooing Darcy's young sister for naught. Her unwavering devotion was his guarantee. His return was to be triumphant—a proud member of the family and brother to the man who had thought of himself as superior.

Now, when I had the means of having it all, I am frustrated by a mere child, and not just any child, but the rotten apple of Darcy's eye. And at a time when my delinquent debts threaten to be the means of my meeting with bodily harm unless I satisfy them by this week's end. Well-chosen words suggesting an alliance with a wealthy young woman who was a recent addition to the neighbourhood would only carry him so far. Thusly had Wickham's charms always served him well when it came to persuading those to whom he owed money to show leniency. Not anymore.

Tapping his foot, he released a long, frustrated breath. *I might serve in the militia for the next decade and hand over every shilling I earn, and it will make no difference.* The thought of suffering another minute in such a life as this with no prospects for escape was untenable. *There is only one thing to do. I must quit the militia.*

Wickham looked at his pocket watch. "Where on earth is that silly bit of muslin?" Before he could fashion his next thought, she came into view. He had no patience for her silliness that particular morning, and as soon as his business with her was done, he wanted to get away. Lydia had other ideas.

"Oh, my dearest Wickham. Our plans are moving along nicely, and what a glorious wedding breakfast I shall have. I can hardly wait! What a great laugh I shall have seeing you there. You must remember to request my hand for a set, for I shall be very sad to see you dance with all the other girls. It is my wedding celebration after all. Oh, and wait until I tell you my good news."

His head was by now swimming. "Well—say what is on your mind."

"I have prevailed upon Mr. Bingley to secure a special license. He insists he will do no such thing, but all his actions thus far have taught me that I need only keep asking and soon he is bound to say yes."

How I wish she could prevail upon that fool Bingley to give her a few hundred pounds that I might use to ward off my creditors.

"How goes your plan to marry Georgiana Darcy? Pray the two of you will not be married until after I am mistress of

Netherfield, for I should hate for everyone's attention to be taken away from my own felicity just yet."

"About that, Lydia—Georgiana and I will not be married after all."

She threw her arms around his neck. "Oh, I just knew you could never marry another when you are so very much in love with me. But how shall we continue to see each other? The militia will not always be in Meryton."

"The truth is that this is the last time we shall ever see each other. My plans have changed, and I no longer intend to be a part of the militia. I am leaving the regiment as soon as can be and setting off for places unknown."

"Oh, I cannot bear the thought of not seeing you. I love you. I adore you. You said that we would always be together—that as soon as I bore Mr. Bingley his heir I would be yours forever."

He removed her arms from his neck with both hands. "The circumstances have changed; however, there is no reason in the world to suppose you shall not be just as happy with Charles Bingley as you might have been with the life we had planned. In fact, this is better for you." *Indeed, it is better for you, but it is absolutely fruitless for me.*

She pressed her hands to his chest. "No—I shall never be happy without you. All the money in the world would be a poor substitute for the way you make me feel when we are together like this. Oh, my dearest Wickham, if you must leave, then you must take me with you."

"Take you with me? Why, I can hardly—" Wickham halted his speech as the wheels of his mind shifted into motion. *This girl is Fitzwilliam Darcy's sister! What a scandal it would be should she and I run away together. There is no telling the measures that pompous arse would undertake to cover up the scandal before the world learns of his family's shame.* The very prospect was enough to revive Wickham's flaccid ardour.

His voice tender and laced with desire, he said, "Why, I can hardly wait." As the two lovers resumed their former attitude, a delighted giggle was next heard.

Chapter 25

Conveying the disturbing news that he had just received from Colonel Forster, the local militia's commanding officer, to Mr. Bennet was the last thing Collins wanted to do. Who was to say how something so alarming, so revolting, would affect the elderly patriarch's recovery? Alas, it must be done. He was, after all, the girl's father. He needed to know, and Collins needed to be the one to tell him.

Mr. Bennet seemed pensive upon hearing what had unfolded under the cover of darkness when the black hearted George Wickham—a man whom Collins had received at Longbourn too many times to count—absconded with the youngest Bennet daughter. Oh, how Collins wanted to believe that the couple had set off for Gretna Green. As scandalous as that would have been, it would have eased the burden of shame a bit. However, all evidence suggested that they were not headed to Scotland. Wickham had confided in his friend, Mr. Denny, that he had other plans for the foolish girl who, by all accounts, had insisted upon fleeing with him. Now equipped with a better understanding of Wickham's vile nature, Collins had no doubt what that meant.

When a full five minutes had passed and still Mr. Bennet had not said a word, Collins began to worry. Had the shock of it all been the undoing of all the progress of the past weeks? His eyes were open, which must surely be a good sign. Collins placed his hand on Mr. Bennet's shoulder. "Sir?"

The look his father-in-law bestowed was confirmation enough for Collins to resume his speech. "It is my place to do all that I can to recover Lydia." Moving away from Mr. Bennet's bedside and drifting towards the window overlooking the garden, he said, "Mine and mine alone."

"Young man, you need not take this burden solely upon yourself," said Mr. Bennet, his voice low and tortured. "It was not you who contributed to her neglect and overindulgence. No, the fault rests solely with me. I ought to suffer for it. Were I able to recover my daughter, I surely would. Even then, I would not take it upon myself to act alone, and you need not either, for you see, you are not alone."

Turning to face his father-in-law, Collins said, "Do you mean to suggest I seek her uncle's assistance? Would you have me solicit Mr. Gardiner's help while I am in town?"

"By all means, for you absolutely must seek my brother's help, but when I say you are not alone, I believe I speak of someone closer in proximity to us."

Collins could not imagine who that would be. *Does he mean Jane? I would rather she did not know the details of any of this sordid affair.* "Sir—"

"Collins, do you not suppose it is time to put aside any differences you still have with Darcy, as well as any misplaced pride?"

"Darcy?"

"Yes, Darcy. He is a good man who cares about his family. To state it more plainly, he cares about all of us. Go and speak with him. He will want to help."

✳ ✳ ✳

Upon entering the room, Elizabeth espied her husband staring out the window overlooking the maze garden. She walked up behind him. He turned and opened his welcoming arms. Accepting his embrace, she smiled. His countenance reflected his continued unrest.

"How is Ben this morning?" said Darcy.

"I would say he is slowly returning to his former self; however, he remains in his room."

It filled her heart with worry that Darcy blamed himself for Ben's low spirits when, in truth, it had everything to do with his uncle's defection. Darcy had not witnessed the effect his own leave-taking from Hertfordshire all those months ago had wrought upon young Ben's state of mind—how he languished about for weeks, thinking he had lost his King Arthur forever.

When Ben loves, he loves with his whole heart and soul. Even though their acquaintance was of a short duration, Elizabeth knew her son was well on his way to loving his uncle Carlton. Both she and Darcy had made it their business to instil in Ben the importance of family, which in theory is always perfect, but in practice can sometimes lead to pain and loss, even suffering. True, Elizabeth wanted to protect her young son from that natural truth, hence her reluctance for him to form an attachment with Henry Carlton, but how unfair it would have been to deny her son the chance to get to know one of the few living relatives on his late father's side of the family.

Darcy diverted his gaze out the window once more. Elizabeth traced her fingers along his chiselled chin. How she loved the feel of his skin. Standing on the tip of her toes, her lips followed the trail of her fingers. "It is not your fault, you know."

"I cannot say that I do."

"You could not have known that Henry Carlton would turn out to be such a disappointment."

"You knew."

"Trust me, my love. I take no pleasure in that."

Their eyes met. Darcy moistened his lips and slowly leaned towards her. Elizabeth closed her eyes and then opened them just as quickly—her hopes interrupted by the sound at the door.

In walked Bingley's butler. He cleared his throat. "Pardon me, Mr. Darcy, Mrs. Darcy. Mr. Geoffrey Collins is here. He requests a private audience with Mr. Darcy."

Darcy and Elizabeth exchanged questioning glances. Darcy said, "Please, send him in."

When the butler stepped outside the room, Elizabeth said, "A private audience with Geoffrey? I wonder what that is about." Her countenance clouded with worry. "You do not suppose—"

Collins entered the room before Elizabeth could complete her sentence. Darcy and she met him halfway across the floor. He bowed slightly. Darcy did likewise and Elizabeth curtsied. "Darcy, Elizabeth," said Collins, "thank you for receiving me."

Elizabeth said, "I shall leave you two to talk."

Collins reached out his hand. "No, Elizabeth, if you would, I wish for you to stay. You see, what I have to say concerns you as well."

Elizabeth placed her hand on her chest. "Pray this has nothing to do with Papa. Has there been a setback in his recovery? When I left him yesterday, he was doing so well."

"No, your father is well, at least as regards his health. But I fear there has been a recent event that threatens not only your father's well-being, but rather the well-being of our entire family." His voice serious, Collins continued, "My news, I fear, is dreadful. You may wish to have a seat."

At that instant, Charles Bingley sauntered into the room. He seemed genuinely surprised to see the three of them standing there. "Oh, pardon my interruption."

"You are not interrupting, Bingley. In fact, I am glad you have come. What I have to discuss with the Darcys concerns you just as much as it does them … in a manner of speaking."

Elizabeth did not like the sound of that at all. She placed her hand on Darcy's arm. Placing his hand over hers, Darcy said, "Shall we all have a seat and hear what Collins has to say?"

When they were all seated, Collins began. "There is no easy way to say this." He ran his fingers through his dark hair. "Lydia … has run away. She has thrown herself into the power of Mr. Wickham."

Elizabeth gasped. *How can this be?* Her eyes followed the same path as her husband's—straight to Bingley's. Before any of them could speak, Collins shot Bingley an apologetic glance and continued to tell them all he had learned about Lydia's shameful behaviour.

After a period of starts and stops, struggling with the words to express his disappointment, Collins turned to Darcy. "You more than anyone know this man. I need your help."

"Of course, I shall do everything in my power to be of service."

"I was hoping you would say that. Lydia and Wickham were said to be off to London. Between the two of us, we ought to be able to recover her before it is too late."

"Indeed. We shall set off for London immediately." Both gentlemen stood.

Bingley said, "I believe I ought to go with the two of you."

The door crashed open and in waltzed Caroline Bingley. As if oblivious to the fact that her brother was not alone, she blurted out, "Charles, I have the most astounding news. It seems my prayers have been answered. Our family is saved."

He coloured. "Caroline, are you completely unaware that we have guests?"

Her face bore none of the contrition that one might expect in such a circumstance as this. "Mr. Collins! I was unaware you were here. I suppose you have come to convey the scandalous turn of events to Mr. Darcy and his *dear* wife."

Charles ran his fingers through his hair. "You know what has happened?"

"My God, Charles, all of Meryton likely knows by now. I knew that little tramp was unworthy of you, and now everyone else knows it too."

"Caroline! How can you be so unfeeling? You will apologise to our guests."

In a tone that belied her true sentiments, she said, "Yes—yes, of course. I do apologise for the shame your youngest sister has brought to your family. Now, if you all will pardon me, I must be away."

"No doubt to spread word of what has befallen the Bennets to everyone else in the county."

"Oh—no! On the contrary, dear brother. I am off to arrange for my return to London as soon as can be. My purpose in remaining in this wretched place for as long as I did was to prevent you from ruining your life. It seems my work is done."

Oh, how Elizabeth was pleased by that bit of information. Once Caroline was gone, she turned to Darcy. Her eyes beaming with unshed tears, she said, "I must be off to Longbourn. My family needs me."

"Of course, my love. I shall come to Longbourn to say goodbye before taking my leave for town."

Collins said, "Elizabeth, you are welcome to join me in the carriage."

"Thank you, Geoffrey."

The decision was then made that Darcy would make arrangements for his and Collins's trip to town. When Collins and Elizabeth had gone, Bingley said, "Darcy, my offer to join in the search for Miss Lydia stands. Despite what this means for me, I really do believe it is the thing to do."

"Charles, I will not try to change your mind. This is a most wretched situation for the family. However, I will understand if you find yourself rejoicing at the outcome. Heaven knows it is a blessing in disguise that young Lydia revealed her true nature before you and she headed to the altar."

When Darcy set off in search of his man in order to arrange his swift departure from Hertfordshire, Bingley took a moment to reflect upon what this twisted turn of events truly meant to him.

How was he meant to feel? *The jilted lover? Fodder for the county's derision?* In truth, he welcomed any manner of ridicule so long as he did not have to marry that foolish Lydia. *If only I could persuade her to retract the malicious accusations staining my character.* Bingley sauntered to the side table and poured himself a drink. He swallowed the amber liquid in one swift gulp. "What does it matter? I am free!"

Triumphant sentiments subsided as the irony of his situation crept into his mind. It might well have been Bingley himself breaking the devastating news to everyone instead of Geoffrey Collins. *I should have gladly traded places with him, for it would mean that Jane was my wife.* How ironic indeed. Bingley now knew what he must do, for the thought of pining away for what would never be was doing him more harm than good. He was a young man with his whole life ahead of him, and he had been given a second chance.

It is time I start acting like it. He cast a nostalgic view around the room. Its greatest ties lay in the fact that it was in this house that he first realised how much he was in love with Jane. *I cannot go on this way. Jane has found love and happiness with another. It is time I do the same. As long as I remain tied to Netherfield, I shall remain tied to Jane.*

"When I return to London, I shall not come back to Hertfordshire. It is time I let Netherfield go."

In love with the notion of being in love, Bingley poured another drink. *Somewhere in all of England there has to be another woman as wonderful as Jane. I shall simply go on hoping and praying that one day I will find an angel I can claim as my own.*

✷ ✷ ✷

As much as the Bennet family would have liked to keep the news of Lydia's scandalous behaviour a secret, it was impossible to keep such a thing concealed. Upon hearing Caroline Bingley agonising over the horrible state of affairs, Georgiana's feelings were a mixture of mortification and astonishment. George Wickham had already proven himself to be less than the man she thought he was by his despicable behaviour towards Ben, but even she never suspected him capable of such mischief as this. *What kind of man would run off with another man's intended?* Her thoughts now tended towards Lydia whom Georgiana always thought of as being rather silly, what with the way she paraded herself before any officer who gave her the slightest bit of encouragement. How she could possibly be Elizabeth's sister was but one of the questions that had raced through Georgiana's mind upon first making Lydia's acquaintance at Pemberley over Christmas.

How could she be so thoughtless as to throw away a promising future life with a man as amicable and caring as Mr. Bingley for the uncertainty that must surely await her with the likes of George Wickham?

That Lydia was young and wild and terribly foolish must surely be her excuse for falling prey to George Wickham's charms. Still, as heartbroken as Georgiana was for the shame that had befallen the Bennet family and, by extension, the Darcy family, she could not help secretly rejoicing that she had not been the means of bringing it about.

Elizabeth came upon Georgiana, who was staring out the window. "Georgiana, I have rather disturbing news to impart. It has to do with my sister Lydia and—"

The younger woman interrupted. "Mr. Wickham?"

"How do you know?"

"I overheard Miss Bingley discussing the matter with her brother."

"I am so sorry. I wanted to be the one to tell you, for I realise how much you admire him."

"Oh, you need not apologise to me. It is true, I did at one time think very highly of Mr. Wickham, but that was before I learned of his true character."

"Pray, what happened?"

"Oh, let us just say a troubling aspect of his character was revealed to me by a dear friend. By the bye, I must thank you for not confiding my misguided secret of thinking so highly of his worst enemy to my brother. I would hate having him know how foolish I was."

"Your secret is safe with me. With that said, I will not promise to always be a party to keeping secrets from my husband."

Georgiana faintly smiled. *Exactly—this is precisely why I hesitate to go into detail of what happened to turn me against Mr. Wickham. I should hate to think what my brother would do if he knew Wickham had threatened to turn Ben over his knee.*

Chapter 26

Count Elizabeth among all those who eagerly awaited the news Geoffrey Collins conveyed the afternoon he returned from town. Lydia had been discovered. She remained in town under the Gardiners' stewardship. Darcy remained in London, as well, to keep watch over Wickham and make certain the scoundrel met Lydia at the altar at the appointed time. Finding the couple had not been as difficult as one would have supposed, not when one had sufficient motives and means. Darcy possessed both. When it was all said and done, Darcy settled untold thousands of pounds in bringing about a more favourable conclusion than any of the Bennet family members had taught themselves to expect.

As distressed as she was in learning that it would be yet some time before Darcy returned, Elizabeth said a silent prayer in appreciation of his sacrifice on behalf of her family.

Upon hearing the news that Lydia was safe and mere days from being married, Mrs. Bennet, who had retired to her sick bed, owing to her grief over the terrible fate that had befallen her youngest daughter, not only found the strength to recover her spirits with breakneck speed, she also found the vigour to boast about her good fortune to all who would listen. Three daughters married and all to such handsome men. Never mind the shame of it all as well as the disgrace that befell poor Mr. Bingley. Everyone who knew the truth of the matter must surely have secretly congratulated him on his good fortune; however, many did not know. Mrs. Bennet blissfully belonged in the latter group. As far as she was concerned, Mr. Bingley's hurt pride was nothing in comparison with the misery he had inflicted upon the Bennets when he treated her Jane so poorly.

Days after the blessed occasion, Mrs. Bennet exclaimed to no one in particular, "Oh, I cannot wait to receive the newlyweds at Longbourn." Clutching her handkerchief, she placed her hand to her head. "I can scarcely believe my brother and sister did not give my Lydia a decent wedding breakfast. We shall make up for such blatant disregard when they come. Oh, there is so much to plan—so much to do." She ceased her frantic prattling and concentrated her attention on her two eldest daughters. "When did you say Lydia and her husband were expected?"

Jane and Elizabeth looked at each other, their eyes filled with concern. Word of Lydia's scandalous behaviour had travelled all the way to Kent, and Jane's brother, Mr. William Collins, wasted no time in making his sentiments known by way of a stern letter to his older brother. With her husband's permission, Jane had shared much of its contents with Elizabeth. The following admonishment, Elizabeth had committed to memory:

"I am truly rejoiced that my cousin Lydia's sad business has been so well hushed up, and am only concerned that their living together before the marriage took place should be so generally known. I must not, however, neglect the duties of my station, nor refrain from declaring my steadfast belief that the young couple must not be admitted into Longbourn even if the union is now sanctioned by marriage. To do so would merely serve as an encouragement of vice, nay a tacit approval. I need not remind you of the poor example this affords to our two unmarried cousins—your own sisters—as well as your own young daughters. You ought certainly to forgive the couple, as a Christian, but never to admit them in your sight or allow their names to be mentioned in your hearing."

Jane said, "Mama, you know Mr. Collins has affirmed that he will not reward Lydia's careless behaviour with a fine wedding breakfast."

"Mr. Collins—Mr. Collins! It is all I ever hear of late. Do his wishes trump my own? Am I not still mistress of my own home? Mr. Collins, indeed."

Elizabeth said, "Mama, it is entirely reasonable that Mr. Collins would feel this way. Lydia's actions made all of us laughing stocks and no one more so than Mr. Bingley. Mr. Wickham's acts were deplorable. Can you blame anyone for feeling that such callous disregard for the feelings of others should not be celebrated?"

"Oh, but what better cause for celebration than a wedding—regardless of how it all came about?" She started towards the door. "I shall speak with Mr. Bennet. Surely he will not condone such heartless treatment of his own daughter."

Jane said, "I wish you would not burden Papa. He is well aware of my husband's sentiments. The two of them are of the same mind."

Disquiet graced the older woman's countenance. "You mean to say that something I have waited for as long as this, to celebrate my youngest daughter's wedding, is not to be? Why, celebrating a daughter's joy of being a new bride is every mother's fondest wish!"

"I am afraid that is exactly what I am saying, Mama."

"Well—we will just see about that," she said.

Both Jane and Elizabeth's protests were insufficient to deter their very determined mother. When Mrs. Bennet was gone, Elizabeth said, "I pray Mama does not tax Papa with her demands. He enjoyed such a pleasant morning. He was sitting by the window looking out at the garden when I visited him. I should hate to think Mama's demands will only upset him."

"Mr. Collins was planning to spend time with Papa later this morning. With any luck, the two of them will be together when Mama arrives in Papa's room aiming to bend him to her will. My husband is adamant that turning a blind eye towards what Lydia has done is out of the question. I should hate to even imagine how Mama will react when she learns from him that Lydia and her husband will not be received at Longbourn."

Her voice a mixture of empathy as well as regret, Elizabeth said, "Speaking of Papa and your husband being of the same mind, I am afraid we must bestow that same distinction upon my own dear husband."

Darcy's first priority upon returning to Hertfordshire was seeing Ben. He hoped to surprise him with his return. After securing his horse, he climbed the stairs to Ben's fortress. "I thought I might find you here."

"Da!" Ben said with greater enthusiasm than Darcy had witnessed in weeks. "I am so happy you are home. Well, I mean to say I am happy you are here."

Darcy stooped to his knees, and Ben and he embraced. "I know what you mean, son. Whenever we are together, regardless of the place, we are home." Ben's tight hold told Darcy that the little fellow had indeed missed him very much. Gently coaxing Ben's arms from about his neck, Darcy took both Ben's hands in his. "What have you been doing while I was away?"

"I have been coming here almost every day, keeping watch over the land. Things have been rather quiet, but I learned the militia is going away, which must explain it."

"Ben, whatever do you mean? How does the militia's being in the environs affect your daily watch? The encampment is far away."

Ben pulled his hands away and tucked them in his pockets. "Oh, I forgot it was meant to be a secret."

"What was meant to be a secret?" Darcy watched Ben's face cloud with indecision. "Ben, I thought you and I did not keep secrets from each other."

"Well, I know we ought not to keep secrets, but in this case it was vital that I say nothing, else I might be guilty of treason."

Treason? What an eager imagination. "I think you ought to let me be the judge of that. After all, treason is a harsh verdict for one as young as you." He brushed his fingers through Ben's unruly curls. "Pray what is this secret you have been keeping all to yourself?"

"I suppose there is no harm in my confiding in you, especially since the secret mission is ended."

"Pray do not keep me in suspense."

"It has to do with Lieutenant Wickham."

Darcy drew a sharp breath at the sound of his former friend's name. "Wickham?"

"Yes, Lieutenant Wickham and Aunt Lydia. I sometimes saw the two of them together."

Darcy closed his eyes and exhaled a worried breath over the prospect of what his son may have witnessed between those two.

Darcy felt the colour rise in his cheeks, and he hoped Ben did not notice his sudden discomfort. Thoughts of the deplorable circumstances in which he had found young Lydia—the filth, the stench, and the bleak despair—flooded his mind. Her attachment to Wickham had been the product of weeks, not days, as Darcy and Collins had taught themselves to believe. *Her scheme to entrap Bingley now makes sense. It was all the product of Wickham's depraved mind.*

"What exactly do you mean when you say you saw them together, Ben?"

Ben raced over to the window and picked up his spyglass. He held it to his eye as he looked out the window. Darcy walked to Ben's side and accepted the proffered instrument. Pointing, Ben said, "I sometimes saw them coming and going together in that area. Aunt Lydia never goes anywhere without Aunt Kitty, and that is why I supposed she was on a secret mission with the militia on behalf of the country."

"So, what you are saying is that you only saw the gentleman and your aunt walking together—nothing more?"

"That is all I ever saw, but as I said, I have seen nothing of the sort since just before you left town. I know that Aunt Lydia has gone away. Is she in town?"

"Ben, I have news about your aunt Lydia. She is in town—or rather she was in London. She has since travelled to Newcastle."

"New castle? Oh, I love castles. Is it very far away? I should very much like to explore it. Shall we journey there for a visit?"

"Yes, Newcastle is far away—very far. It is not exactly a castle, but rather a town in the north. However, we shall not be travelling there." *God willing.* "You see, your aunt is not alone. She is recently married—to George Wickham."

"But ... but..." Pausing to fashion his thoughts, Ben bit his lower lip. "I have a new uncle? Does this mean that we no longer hate him?"

"Hate is a very strong emotion, Ben. Dislike, distrust—I feel both of these sentiments are more fitting."

"No—I was rather certain we hated him."

"It is complicated, Ben. You know that George Wickham and I were the closest of friends at one time. However, as we grew older he proved himself to be deplorable. I never wanted anything to do with him, and I certainly never wanted him anywhere near our family."

"Now he is my uncle. He is our family."

"Your uncle and my brother." Darcy nearly choked on the appellations. "We must endeavour to tolerate him." *The prospects of which are tenable with the promise that it will be a long time before we lay eyes on him again.*

"Da, may I ask you a question?"

"Of course you may, son."

"You said that you and the lieutenant were the best of friends when you were young, but then he did something to cause you to hate him. Is that the reason you do not like Samuel?"

"Ben, I do not dislike Samuel."

"Well, you do not like him either."

"No ... well, yes..." After a couple of starts and stops attempting to clarify his stance, Darcy said, "Samuel is nothing at all like my former friend. He is a good person—honest and trustworthy—and I am sorry I gave you the impression I felt otherwise."

"But do you like him?"

"Yes, Ben. I like him very much. You are fortunate to have such a friend."

"Oh, Da! I am delighted to hear you say that, for I have missed Samuel more and more each day. I am so sad he will never see my fortress."

"It is not too late for you to share all this with Samuel."

"Do you mean to say that the next time we visit Hertfordshire Samuel will come with us?"

"Actually, I was thinking we might reconstruct all this at Pemberley—the three of us."

Ben's brightened countenance reminded Darcy of that which he had missed most over the past weeks.

"That is the greatest news, ever! Oh, I can hardly wait," said Ben.

Ben's enthusiasm also reminded Darcy of another thing that he longed for: returning to his beloved home with his family. They had been away for far too long. Darcy and Ben embraced. "Neither can I, son. Neither can I."

Elizabeth was not at Netherfield Park when Darcy arrived with Ben in tow. He rightly supposed she was at Longbourn. When she arrived, hearing the news of all that had transpired while he was away was uppermost in her mind. The subject of the newlyweds and all the disapprobation their situation entailed nearly exhausted, Elizabeth sought a more agreeable discussion. "You mentioned that the colonel was involved in your recovery of my sister."

"Indeed, Richard proved quite instrumental in helping to persuade Wickham to remain in town as his wedding day approached."

"Then I must express my gratitude to him as well. Did he say whether his plans would bring him back to Hertfordshire?"

"No. I imagine we will not see him again until Christmas."

"Oh, dear! How does that affect your hopes for an alliance between him and Anne?"

Widening his eyes, Darcy said, "Were my wishes in that regard so obvious?"

"Indeed, my dear husband. I am afraid you are an unabashed matchmaker."

"One might argue I am not a very good matchmaker."

"Do you speak of your unsuccessful attempt with Anne and Richard, or your disappointment as regards Georgiana and Bingley?"

"I do not deny that both matches would have suited me but, alas, it seems neither is destined to be. Georgiana and Bingley scarcely acknowledge the other exists, and while I believe Anne may have welcomed Richard's attention, he does not feel the same. He never has, and I doubt he ever will."

"If it helps you recover from your disappointed hopes, I would say that any disappointment that Anne may have suffered in that regard is a thing of the past."

"Did she tell you that?"

"Indeed, soon after Richard took his leave of Hertfordshire, she and I discussed the matter at length."

"It warms my heart that you and Cousin Anne can speak freely on such matters. While she is at liberty to remain a part of our family circle for as long as she wishes, I do hope that she will find the happiness that comes with being the mistress of her own home."

Elizabeth placed her hand against his cheek. "Fear not, my love, for you have next Season to make matches for all four of them—Anne, Georgiana, Richard, and Bingley."

Darcy took Elizabeth's hand in his and brushed a kiss against her knuckles. "I think not. From this point on, I shall think only of my own advantageous alliance, if it is all the same to you."

Elizabeth smiled. "Indeed, I like the sound of that."

He led his wife to the sofa and persuaded her to sit beside him. He swept his fingers through her loosened hair. "The Gardiners asked me to give you their best wishes."

"Thank you, my love. I have not kept up with my writing to them as I ought. I do miss them so."

"Then you will be delighted by my next pronouncement."

"Oh, do tell."

"You will recall that your aunt has acquaintances in Lambton."

"I did not know you were aware of that."

"Indeed. I had ample opportunity to visit with the Gardiners, what with the part they had in accommodating your sister during the days leading up to the wedding."

"Again, you must allow me to thank you for the mortification that must have attended the task of recovering my sister."

"You have no need to thank me. You are my wife, which makes Lydia my sister."

Elizabeth placed her hand upon his and squeezed it gently.

Darcy said, "You have not heard my happy news."

"Pray proceed, and this time I shall not interrupt you. I promise."

"Mrs. Gardiner informed me that they planned a trip to the Lakes later in the summer when her husband's business will allow for travel. She said they planned to call on acquaintances in Lambton as well. Once I was in company with Mr. Gardiner, I prevailed upon him to visit Pemberley. I knew not what to expect in light of our prior disagreement over the financial management of your trust, but he accepted my invitation."

"How wonderful! This means my aunt and uncle will finally have an opportunity to see Pemberley and to be welcomed there as members of the family and not merely tourists. Oh, how I wish they would bring the children and perhaps even allow them to stay with us while they continue on to the Lakes. Can you imagine what that would mean to Ben to have so many people of his own age running about the halls with him?"

"I should imagine he would love the chance to do just that."

"On the other hand, I can well imagine what a challenge it would be for my aunt and uncle to travel all that way with four small children."

"Well, do not rule out the possibility based solely upon conjecture."

"You raise a valid point. I must write to my aunt at once to ascertain her thoughts on the scheme." Elizabeth stood and then immediately returned to her seat. "Of course, all this means that we shall soon be leaving Hertfordshire."

"Your father is much recovered, and the situation is resolved with your sister. I do feel the time has come for us to return to Derbyshire; although I have no wish to rush you into anything."

"My father is indeed recovering. It meant so much to me to be here during the time when he needed me most. I take comfort in the fact that all of our past differences have been cast aside, and he and I have both embraced my philosophy to only think of the past as its remembrance brings us pleasure."

"It is a wise philosophy, indeed. In fact, I believe Collins and I are of the same mind. I believe he and I made great strides in understanding each other when we were forced to be in each other's company in town."

"That is wonderful, especially as he has my father's blessing to take over the active management of the Longbourn estate."

"How do you truly feel about that situation?"

"I believe it is for the best. As much as I love and revere Papa, if I am to be completely honest, I would have to say he did not govern the estate as well as he ought, and now he need not give such matters any further thought. Already I have seen positive evidence of Geoffrey's stewardship of Longbourn. I am sure my family's future is in good hands."

Chapter 27

The Darcys returned to Netherfield after what was to be their last evening at Longbourn during their stay. Alone in their apartment, Elizabeth placed her arms around Darcy's neck, resting her head on his chest as he moved to enfold her in his arms. "May I commend you for holding your tongue when Mama mentioned Lydia's letter stating how much she looks forward to visiting Pemberley at Christmas with her new husband?"

Biting his tongue was more like it. Darcy swore he tasted blood. "I saw no need to broach the subject with your mother, further upsetting her over the prospect of not seeing Lydia for who knows how long. However, you must know that I have no intention of ever receiving Wickham in my home, especially not after what he has done." Darcy recalled how appalled Elizabeth was, and rightfully so, when he shared his suspicion that Wickham had violated her sister weeks before stealing away with her. Softening his stance, he said, "As for whether your sister is received, that is entirely up to you."

"After what those two have done, the damage to our family's reputation as well as Mr. Bingley's, I understand your sentiments perfectly well. However, Lydia is my sister. I do not think that I could ever completely turn my back on her."

"I say we do not give the matter another thought, at least not tonight."

"Then, what shall we discuss?"

"There is one thing I wish to mention. I have been giving some thought to speaking with Mr. Coolidge about adjusting his lesson plans."

"Pray this means you have reconsidered your stance against Samuel's presence in the classroom with Ben."

"I feel I must. Ben's friendship with Samuel is important to him. Their camaraderie brings so much joy to Ben's days. I want Ben to enjoy his childhood for as long as he can, without thoughts of his place in society, his future responsibility as a landed gentleman and all that comes with such privilege. If having Ben's friend enjoy some of the same privileges is the means of bringing that about, then so be it."

"You amaze me, my love." She lightly placed her hand on her stomach. "Pray does this philosophy also apply to the future heir of Pemberley?"

Her innocent gesture gave him cause to wonder whether his wife was speaking hypothetically or if there was something he ought to know. However, in light of their tacit agreement to eschew talk of any such matters that might give rise to disappointed hopes, he decided not to press her. All would unfold when the time was right. He reached for Elizabeth's hand, raised it to his lips and brushed a kiss across her knuckles before continuing his speech.

"Indeed it does. Of course, this is the direct opposite of how my father taught me to regard my role as his heir. When the time comes, if I should falter, I shall expect you to help me along the way."

"You can have no doubt I will do just that. Speaking of your father, I take it that you have no more concerns about the great sins of elevating young Samuel beyond the sphere into which he was born?"

"Having witnessed my father's mistakes first-hand, I have a good idea of which ones to avoid. However, I trust you will help me with that as well."

"Indeed." Elizabeth's countenance brightened. "I can think of one person, other than Ben and Samuel, who will be delighted by your change of heart."

"Who else?"

"Why, Mrs. Reynolds, of course. Oh, I know what she said about everyone having their place, but what grandmother would not relish such opportunity for her grandchild?"

✶ ✶ ✶

The following week, the Darcys' travels saw them arrive safely in Derbyshire once more. After so many months away, the collective spirit in the procession of fine carriages was one and the same. Pemberley—how good it was to be home again.

Elizabeth's prediction proved true as regarded the impact of Darcy's change of heart on Mrs. Reynolds, for upon hearing of her master's new-found philosophy, Mrs. Reynolds's pleasure could not be repressed. She more than just thanked

Mr. Darcy for his benevolence towards her only grandchild; she embraced him with open arms.

The last time Mrs. Reynolds, who was more like a mother to him than not, had embraced him was when he returned from Cambridge for the first time. Her simple act of kindness meant more to Darcy than she could ever know. While watching her quit the room, a not too distant moment came to mind—the day he and his family returned to Pemberley.

Many of the household servants had stood in line to welcome the family, young Samuel included among them. Breaking with decorum, he raced towards Ben as soon as Ben descended his carriage. The two hurried off towards the stables.

As excited as Ben was to be reunited with his friend, mid-stride, he spun about on his heels and tore off in Darcy's direction. Darcy caught his son. He lifted Ben high in the sky. Heartfelt joy and laughter filled the air. When Darcy lowered him, Ben threw both arms around Darcy's neck. He clung to him. "Thank you, Father!"

Darcy's eyes sought Ben's. "*Father?* Pray you are not vexed, my son."

"Oh, no! I am happier than ever."

"Yet, you just called me—"

"Father—I know, as I shall call you forever more, for you are my father." Ben rested his head on Darcy's shoulder. "I have the best father in all the land."

The Author

P. O. Dixon is a writer as well as an entertainer. Historical England and its days of yore fascinate her. She, in particular, loves the Regency period with its strict mores and oh so proper decorum. Her ardent appreciation of Jane Austen's timeless works set her on the writer's journey. Dixon delights in weaving diverting tales of gallant gentlemen on horseback and the women they love. Visit podixon.com and find out more about Dixon's writing endeavors.

Connect with the Author Online

Blog: http://podixon.blogspot.com
Twitter: @podixon
Facebook: http://www.facebook.com/podixon
Pinterest: http://pinterest.com/podixon
Website: http://podixon.com
Email: podixon@podixon.com

Author's Books

§ **Pride and Prejudice Untold Series:**

- To Have His Cake (and Eat It Too): Mr. Darcy's Tale (Book 1)
- What He Would Not Do: Mr. Darcy's Tale Continues (Book 2)
- Lady Harriette: Fitzwilliam's Heart and Soul (Book 3)

§ **Darcy and the Young Knight's Quest Series:**

- He Taught Me to Hope (Book 1)
- The Mission: He Taught Me to Hope Christmas Vignette (Book 2)
- Hope and Sensibility (Book 3)

Other Pride and Prejudice "What-if" Stories:

- A Lasting Love Affair: Darcy and Elizabeth
- Still a Young Man: Darcy Is In Love
- Bewitched, Body and Soul: Miss Elizabeth Bennet
- Matter of Trust: The Shades of Pemberley
- Love Will Grow: A Pride and Prejudice Story
- Only a Heartbeat Away: Pride and Prejudice Novella
- Almost Persuaded: Miss Mary King
- Pride and Sensuality: A Darcy and Elizabeth Short Story

Made in the USA
San Bernardino, CA
21 March 2015